WE STILL EXIST.

ADVIK SINHA

Contents

About The Author

Advik Sinha, a twelve-year-old student at Bhavan Vidyalaya in New Chandigarh, is a passionate science fiction enthusiast who devours books across various genres. His love for reading is only matched by his fervor for writing, a passion that has culminated in the creation of his debut book, which you are currently holding.

Residing in Chandigarh, India, Advik Sinha lives with his parents, nurturing his imagination and literary ambitions. His journey into the realm of storytelling began with a fascination for science fiction, fueling his creative spirit and inspiring him to craft compelling narratives that captivate readers of all ages.

Feel free to reach him at any time at en.advik.sinha@gmail.com

Preface

In the vast expanse of the cosmos, where stars blink into existence and galaxies dance in eternal spirals, humanity has always looked to the heavens with wonder and curiosity. Our journey into the unknown, fueled by a relentless thirst for knowledge and discovery, has led us to the edges of our solar system and beyond.

This book chronicles the extraordinary odyssey of the AWSRA team—a group of daring scientists and explorers who ventured beyond the familiar confines of Earth to uncover the mysteries of our origins. Their mission, codenamed "Origins," began with a bold quest: to establish contact with a distant planet, H1009b, believed to harbor the remnants of ancient human civilizations.

Through wormholes and encounters with enigmatic alien species, the AWSRA team navigated the challenges of space-time itself, driven by a singular purpose—to connect with our distant ancestors and forge a path towards interstellar cooperation.

Their journey is a testament to the resilience of the human spirit, the power of scientific inquiry, and the unyielding belief in the potential of collaboration across cosmic distances. As we stand on the precipice of an era where the boundaries of space and time blur, their story serves as both a beacon of hope and a call to embrace the limitless possibilities that await us among the stars.

Join us as we embark on a voyage through the cosmos—a journey that explores the depths of human ingenuity, the bonds that unite us across galaxies, and the profound mysteries that define our place in the universe.

Join us in this gripping tale of resilience, innovation, and the fight for a future. Welcome to "WE STILL EXIST."

Introduction

In the year 2088, Earth teeters on the brink of ecological collapse. Climate change has ravaged the planet, leaving humanity facing its greatest challenge yet. Amidst this turmoil, Dr. Aviyan Murphy emerges as a beacon of hope, leading the Earth Welfare Society (EWS) in a desperate bid to save our world.

"WE STILL EXIST" chronicles the extraordinary efforts of Dr. Murphy and his team as they navigate this critical juncture in human history. Their journey is a testament to the enduring spirit of humanity and our unyielding resolve to survive against all odds.

"Sometimes I think we're alone in the universe, and sometimes I think we're not. In either case, the idea is quite staggering."- Arthur C. Clarke

Prologue

In the hazy glow of the year 2088, Earth found itself teetering on the brink of catastrophe. Rampant climate change has unfurled its cruel tendrils across the globe, rendering once-vibrant ecosystems barren and inhospitable. As temperatures soared and sea levels surged, the very fabric of life on the planet seemed to unravel before humanity's eyes.

Amidst this turmoil, Dr. Aviyan Murphy emerged as a beacon of hope in the darkness, his name whispered in revered tones among the corridors of power and the halls of science. A figure of singular brilliance, his dual expertise in astrophysics and biology positioned him as a guiding force within the Earth Welfare Society (EWS), an organization tasked with safeguarding the planet and its inhabitants.

With every furrow of his brow and every word that fell from his lips, Dr. Murphy exuded an aura of authority tempered by compassion. His piercing gaze, framed by the lines of wisdom etched upon his face, held within it the weight of a thousand stars—each one a testament to the vast expanse of his intellect and the depths of his resolve.

When the time came for humanity to confront its greatest trial, Dr. Murphy stood at the forefront, a steadfast bulwark against the encroaching tide of despair. In a pivotal meeting with Earth's leaders, he delivered a stark ultimatum, his voice a clarion call to action amidst the cacophony of uncertainty.

"We stand on the precipice of extinction," he declared, his words ringing out with a clarity that brooked no dissent. "But in our unity lies our salvation. We must act swiftly and decisively if we are to secure a future for ourselves and for generations yet unborn."

Thus began a race against time—a symphony of logistics and coordination orchestrated by Dr. Murphy's steady hand. With the weight of 7.2 billion souls resting heavy upon his shoulders, he marshaled every resource at his disposal, drawing upon the collective ingenuity of humanity to fashion a lifeline amidst the chaos.

In the frenzied blur of the ensuing month, continents trembled beneath the thunderous roar of rocket engines. As humanity embarked on a journey into the unknown, Each vessel, a testament to human resilience and determination, bore within it the hopes and dreams of a species on the brink of extinction.

And as the last echoes of humanity faded into the void, Dr. Murphy stood on the precipice of history, a solitary figure gazing out across the vast expanse of space. In the silence that followed, he whispered a silent prayer—a fervent plea for redemption and a solemn vow to never forget the world they had left behind.

For in their departure, humanity had bequeathed to Earth a final legacy—a message encoded within the very fabric of life itself (DNA). A message that spoke of resilience in the face of adversity and of the enduring spirit of exploration that defines us as a species.

And though the stars may have beckoned with their siren song, Dr. Murphy knew that Earth would forever remain the cradle of humanity—a beacon of hope amidst the infinite expanse of the cosmos.

ONE

WE STILL EXIST!

"*In the year 34,000 A.D., Earth was home to the Novans, a highly advanced species that had evolved from ancient humans. These beings lived in harmony with their environment, guided by the teachings and myths passed down through countless generations. Among the Novans, the ancient humans were revered as divine ancestors, worshipped for their wisdom and the legacy they left behind.*"

The tension in the Outer Space Exploration Hall, located in AWSRA Building No. 2, had been palpable for days. A weak signal had been emanating from an anonymous location in the galaxy, puzzling scientists and sparking speculation about its origin.

"01010111 01000101 00100000 01010011 01010100 01001001 01001100 01001100 00100000 010001 01 01011000 01001001 01010011 01010100, We have got a mysterious signal from space," announced Dr. Arius Nova to her colleagues.

"WE STILL EXIST" one of her colleagues exclaimed, realizing the significance of the message. The entire hall fell into a thoughtful silence as they pondered its meaning.

"Dr. Arius Nova was a distinguished scientist, holding a prominent position within the All World Space Research Alliance (AWSRA). Renowned for her groundbreaking contributions to space research and astrophysics, Dr. Nova was a pivotal figure in the global scientific community."

Excitement and confusion filled the faces of everyone in the hall as they speculated about the true meaning behind the message. Suddenly, Dr. Arius remembered a discovery from a previous expedition—a message encoded in DNA that also proclaimed, "WE STILL EXIST. SOMEWHERE IN THIS GALAXY, WE LIVED HERE A LONG TIME BEFORE YOU. IF YOU FOUND THIS, YOU ARE A VERY LUCKY CIVILIZATION."

Dr. Nova recounted the discovery to her colleagues, explaining how they had found a bottle containing the intricate designs of DNA-encoded messages years ago.

Upon hearing this revelation, the scientists were stunned. "Could it be them?" whispered Professor Lyra, a historian who had dedicated her life to studying ancient human texts and artifacts. "Could our ancestors still be out there?"

The idea was both thrilling and daunting. If true, it meant that the ancient legends of humans venturing into the cosmos were not mere myths but historical truths. Determined to uncover the truth, Dr. Arius and her team resolved to trace the origin of the signal.

After deliberating on their next steps, the scientists unanimously agreed to escalate the matter to higher authorities. Dr. Arius swiftly arranged an emergency meeting with the government and AWSRA, scheduled for 2:00 PM. With the time ticking away until the meeting, Dr. Arius found herself in the cafeteria during the lunch break, where she was joined by Dr. Lyra Nova, a prominent colleague. Dr. Lyra was so thrilled by what happened in the hall; it was like her dream come true.

As they sat together, sipping their drinks and discussing the implications of the mysterious signal, Dr. Lyra's eyes sparkled with excitement. "Imagine what this discovery could mean for our understanding of human history," she mused. "We could be on the brink of uncovering a truth that has been hidden for millennia."

Dr. Arius nodded in agreement, her mind racing with possibilities. The journey ahead would be fraught with challenges and uncertainties, but she knew that they were on the cusp of something extraordinary. With the echoes of ancient legends guiding their way, they embarked on a quest to unlock the secrets of humanity's past and unravel the mysteries of the cosmos.

Little did they know, their journey would not only lead them to the answers they sought but also to revelations that would forever change their understanding of the universe and humanity's place within it.

But for now, as they sat in the bustling cafeteria, surrounded by the chatter of their fellow scientists and the hum of activity, they allowed themselves to bask in the excitement of the moment, knowing that they were on the verge of embarking on a journey that would shape the course of history.

Their conversation was interrupted by the arrival of Dr. Rian Dax, a leading expert in exobiology. "Mind if I join you?" he asked, holding a tray with a simple sandwich and a cup of tea.

"Of course, Rian," Arius replied, gesturing to the empty seat next to Lyra. "We were just discussing the signal and its potential implications."

Rian set his tray down and took a seat, his expression thoughtful. "The signal is binary, but it carries a deeper message. 'We still exist.' It's both a declaration and an invitation. But why now? Why after all these years?"

Lyra's eyes sparkled with curiosity. "Perhaps they were waiting for us to reach a certain level of advancement. Or maybe it's a distress signal. Either way, we need to find out."

Arius glanced at her watch. "We have about an hour before the emergency meeting. We should use this time to prepare our findings and present a compelling case to the government and AWSRA."

Rian nodded in agreement. "I'll gather the data from our recent signal analyses. Lyra, can you compile the historical context and previous discoveries related to ancient humans?"

"Already on it," Lyra said, tapping on her tablet to bring up her extensive notes and research materials.

As they worked, the cafeteria's noise faded into the background; their focus was solely on the task at hand. The minutes ticked by quickly, and soon it was time to head to the meeting in just 34 minutes.

Dr. Arius Nova, along with Dr. Lyra Nova and Dr. Rian Dax, hurried to the conference hall. Their minds raced as they went over the final details of their presentation. They were about to present one of the most significant discoveries in human history, and the weight of this responsibility was not lost on them.

Upon entering the conference hall, they were met with a flurry of activity. The technicians were setting up the projection screens and ensuring the audio-visual equipment was functioning correctly. The room, with its sleek design and state-of-the-art technology, buzzed with a palpable sense of anticipation.

"Let's get the presentation loaded," Arius instructed, her voice calm but authoritative. Lyra connected her tablet to the main display, bringing up the slides they had meticulously prepared. Rian checked the audio levels, ensuring that their voices would carry clearly to every corner of the spacious room.

The clock was ticking—just 5 minutes left. The trio worked in synchrony, their movements precise and efficient. Arius glanced at the agenda displayed on the wall-mounted screen, mentally preparing herself for the questions and discussions that would follow their presentation.

One by one, the government officials began to file in. They were accompanied by senior scientists, representatives from various space agencies, and members of the press. The gravity of the occasion was evident in their serious expressions and hushed conversations.

Arius took a deep breath, her eyes scanning the room. She spotted Director Elena Vos, head of AWSRA, entering with a group of high-ranking officials. Their presence underscored the importance of the meeting, adding another layer of pressure.

The scientists and staff settled down, the room gradually falling into a focused silence. Arius, Lyra, and Rian stood at the front, ready to present their findings. The large screen behind them displayed the first slide: a visual representation of the mysterious signal, its binary code prominently featured.

Director Vos called the meeting to order. "Ladies and gentlemen, thank you for gathering on such short notice. We have a matter of great importance to discuss today. Dr. Arius Nova and her team have made a discovery that could potentially change our understanding of human history. Dr. Nova, you have the floor."

Arius stepped forward, her heart pounding but her voice steady. "Thank you, Director Vos. Esteemed colleagues and officials, today we are here to discuss a signal we have recently detected. This signal, emanating from an unknown location in the galaxy, contains a message that reads, 'We still exist.'"

She paused to let the weight of her words sink in. The room was silent, with every eye on her and every mind processing the implications.

Arius continued, "This message, in binary code, matches the pattern of an ancient message we discovered years ago, encoded in DNA. That message read, 'WE STILL EXIST. Somewhere in this galaxy, we lived here a long time before you. IF YOU FOUND THIS, YOU ARE A VERY LUCKY CIVILIZATION.' We believe these two messages are connected and indicate that our ancient human ancestors might still be out there."

Lyra took over, her voice filled with passion as she provided the historical context. "Our *ancestors, whom we revere as divine beings, might have ventured into space long ago. This signal could be a direct link to them, confirming that they survived and have been observing us. This discovery could rewrite our understanding of human history and our place in the cosmos."*

The presentation continued, with Rian explaining the technical aspects of the signal. "The complexity of the signal suggests an advanced technology far beyond our current capabilities. This implies that our ancestors achieved a level of technological sophistication that we have yet to comprehend fully."

The room remained silent as the implications of their findings sank in. The officials and scientists exchanged glances, their expressions ranging from astonishment to deep contemplation.

Arius concluded the presentation. "We propose a dedicated mission to trace the origin of this signal. Such an endeavor would not only uncover our history but could also lead to unprecedented advancements in science and technology."

Director Vos stood again, her face thoughtful. "Thank you, Dr. Nova, Dr. Lyra, and Dr. Dax. Your findings are indeed remarkable. We will now open the floor for questions and discussions."

Hands shot up around the room as officials and scientists sought to understand more about the potential mission.

Dr. Rian Dax *stood, addressing the assembled officials and scientists. His focus shifted to* **President Samantha Turner,** *the head of the global united government.*

Dr. Dax: *"President Turner, given the significant implications and potential risks associated with this mission, we understand the need for comprehensive government oversight and support. May I ask what specific concerns or priorities the government has regarding this mission? How can we ensure our objectives align with national and international interests?"*

President Turner listened attentively, his expression thoughtful. He understood the gravity of the situation and the unprecedented nature of the mission. After a moment of contemplation, he responded.

President Turner: "Dr. Dax, thank you for bringing this up. Our primary concerns are the safety of the project, the protection of civilization, and the ethical considerations surrounding any potential contact with advanced beings. Additionally, we must consider how to handle and disseminate the information to the public to avoid unnecessary panic or misinformation. Your team's expertise and preparedness will be crucial in addressing these concerns."

Dr. Dax nodded, appreciating the president's candid response. He continued.

Dr. Dax: "Thank you, President Turner. We have indeed developed comprehensive safety protocols and risk mitigation strategies. We also have a clear plan for resource allocation to ensure other projects remain unaffected. As for ethical considerations and public communication, we have engaged experts in these fields to guide us. We will maintain transparency with the government and the public, ensuring the *responsible and controlled dissemination of information. Your support will be invaluable in achieving these goals."*

President Turner *smiled approvingly.*

President Turner: *"I am reassured by your thorough approach, Dr. Dax. The government's role will be to facilitate your efforts, provide the necessary support, and ensure that the mission aligns with our broader objectives. You have our full backing for this historic endeavor."*

President Turner: *"We allow you and your team to work on this project to your full potential. We hope for the success of this intricate project. Best of luck!"*

President Turner's words resonated with Dr. Dax and his team, instilling confidence and determination as they embarked on this historic mission. With a respectful nod, Dr. Dax acknowledged the president's support.

Dr. Dax: *"Thank you, President Turner. Your trust and support mean a great deal to us. Rest assured, we will devote ourselves fully to this endeavor, striving to unlock the mysteries of our* *past and push the boundaries of human exploration. We are grateful for the opportunity to contribute to the advancement of our collective knowledge and understanding. We will make every effort to ensure the success of this intricate project. Thank you for your confidence in us."*

Dr. Arius: *"Ladies and gentlemen, we appreciate your engagement and thoughtful questions. Allow us to address any remaining doubts and provide further clarification on our mission objectives and strategies."*

Dr. Lyra: *"The scientific and historical evidence supporting our endeavor is robust and compelling. We have meticulously planned every aspect of the mission to ensure its success, drawing on the expertise of our multidisciplinary team and leveraging cutting-edge technology."*

Dr. Rian: *"Furthermore, we have developed contingency plans for every conceivable scenario, prioritizing the safety of the crew and the integrity of the mission. With your continued support and collaboration, we are confident that we can achieve our goals and uncover the truth hidden within the cosmos."*

As the trio elaborated on their plans and addressed the remaining concerns, a sense of excitement and anticipation filled the room. The officials nodded in agreement, impressed by the thoroughness and dedication of the scientists.

President Turner: "Thank you, Dr. Arius, Dr. Lyra, and Dr. Rian, for your comprehensive responses. It's evident that you have put a tremendous amount of thought and effort into this mission. On behalf of the government and the global community, I commend you for your dedication and vision. We look forward to witnessing the results of your groundbreaking research."

"With the doubts dispelled and the officials fully briefed, the stage was set for the next phase of the mission. The trio's meticulous planning and unwavering commitment had earned them the confidence and support of the highest authorities, paving the way for humanity's most ambitious journey yet."

And soon, as all the officials started to leave the hall on their way back, the trio gathered and decided to form a team and make further plans for this mission.

"The conference went very well, as expected by all of us," Dr. Dax remarked, his tone reflecting a mix of relief and excitement.

Dr. Arius and Dr. Lyra nodded in agreement, sharing the sentiment. They could feel the weight of responsibility lifting off their shoulders as the officials departed, leaving behind an atmosphere charged with anticipation for the mission ahead.

"Indeed, it exceeded our expectations," Dr. Arius chimed in, a smile tugging at the corners of her lips. "Now, it's time to take the next steps. We need to assemble a team and delve deeper into our plans for this mission."

Dr. Lyra nodded, her mind already whirling with thoughts of potential team members and logistical considerations. "Agreed. We'll need to identify individuals with the right expertise and skillsets to complement our own. And we must ensure that our plans are thorough and meticulously thought out."

"With renewed determination, the trio set off to strategize and make preparations for the next phase of their journey. They knew that the road

ahead would be challenging, but they were ready to face whatever obstacles came their way. After all, they were on the verge of embarking on a mission that could reshape humanity's understanding of its place in the universe."

TWO
TEAM AND PLAN

The departure of the officials marked a turning point. With the support and authorization from the highest authorities, Dr. Arius Nova, Dr. Lyra Nova, and Dr. Rian Dax stood on the precipice of an unprecedented journey. They returned to their offices, each brimming with ideas and plans.

In the quiet of the planning room, Dr. Arius was the first to break the silence. "Now that we have the green light, it's time to build a team that can turn this vision into reality."

Dr. Lyra, flipping through her notes, nodded. "We need to identify the best minds in various fields: astrophysics, genetics, engineering, and more. This mission will require a multidisciplinary approach."

Dr. Rian added, "And we must also consider operational logistics. We'll need experienced spacecraft engineers, navigators, and medical professionals to ensure the crew's health and safety during the mission."

The trio spent the next few hours drafting a list of potential candidates. They reached out to universities, research institutions, and space agencies worldwide. Their criteria were strict: the chosen few needed to be not only experts in their fields but also capable of working under the high-pressure conditions of deep-space exploration.

Dr. Arius sent an urgent message to Dr. Elena Garcia, a renowned engineer at the International Space Agency known for her work on advanced propulsion systems. Her expertise would be crucial in designing a spacecraft capable of reaching the signal's origin.

Meanwhile, Dr. Lyra contacted Dr. Sarah Dax, Director of the Global Space Research Council, to seek recommendations for leading geneticists and biologists. The connection between the signal and the ancient DNA-encoded message needed thorough investigation.

Dr. Rian reached out to Dr. Marcus Dax, Professor of Advanced Engineering at the University of Advanced Engineering, to delve deeper into the logical and engineered context and artifacts that might shed light on the ancient humans' technology.

Responses came quickly. Enthusiasm was high among the scientific community, with many eager to join what promised to be the most significant mission of their careers. Within a week, a team of distinguished experts from around the globe was assembled, each member bringing their unique skills and knowledge to the table.

As the team gathered at AWSRA's headquarters, the atmosphere was electric. Introductions were made, and the room buzzed with discussions about their respective fields and how they could contribute to the mission.

Dr. Elena Nova spoke first, her eyes gleaming with excitement. "I've been working on a new propulsion system that could significantly cut down travel time. With some modifications, it could be perfect for this mission."

Dr. Sarah Dax added, "Understanding the genetic message will be key. We need to decode it thoroughly to comprehend the ancient humans' intentions and capabilities."

Dr. Marcus Dax, poring over historical texts, said, "I am very excited to test all the designs and functionality of all the equipment."

"Finally, congratulations to all of us; we have formed a team of top-notch minds in all the fields." Dr. Arius remarked, addressing every member of the team.

Name Role Expertise

Dr. Arius Nova Lead Scientist Research and Astrophysics

Dr. Lyra Nova Historian Ancient Human Texts and Artifacts

Dr. Rian Dax Project Coordinator Space Mission Planning and Coordination

Dr. Elena Nova Propulsion Engineer Advanced Propulsion Systems

Dr. Sarah Dax biologist Genetic Analysis

Dr. Marcus Dax Engineer Designing and Functionality

"Very well, now we must give a name to this project." Suggested by Dr. Rian Dax

"Yes, sure, we must give a name to the project." Said Dr. Arius Nova

"What about... um,ORIGIN' " Said Dr. Arius

"Perfect, let's ask everybody first if they satisfy."

"Ok," said Dr. Arius.

"They asked Dr. Lyra, Dr. Elena, Dr. Sarah, and Dr. Marcus; everyone was satisfied and happy with this name."

"Okay, so from now on, we will call this project 'ORIGINS'." Said Dr. Rian Dax

"The collaboration between these brilliant minds laid the foundation for the mission. The team knew that their journey would be fraught with challenges and uncertainties. But the promise of uncovering humanity's ancient past and its place in the cosmos filled them with a sense of purpose and excitement. They were ready to embark on an extraordinary mission, one that would shape the future and redefine their understanding of history."

Later that night, Dr. Rian Dax found himself lying in bed, staring at the ceiling. The events of the day played over and over in his mind. They had made significant progress, yet the weight of the mission's potential rested heavily on his shoulders.

"Ah, why am I not even able to sleep?" he muttered to himself. The excitement of the project, coupled with the enormity of its implications, kept his mind racing.

He sat up and reached for his tablet on the bedside table. Maybe reviewing some of the data would help clear his thoughts. As he scrolled through the latest updates from the propulsion team, a message from Dr. Arius caught his eye.

"Rian, I know it's late, but I wanted to share my thoughts. This mission is monumental, and I feel the same restlessness you do. Let's meet early tomorrow to go over the next steps. – Arius"

Rian smiled. It was comforting to know he wasn't alone in his sleeplessness. He replied, "Thanks, Arius. I'll be in the office at 6 a.m. Let's make sure we cover everything."

Setting the tablet aside, he decided to make himself a cup of herbal tea. As he waited for the water to boil, he gazed out of the window at the night sky. The stars seemed brighter tonight, as if they too were eager for the journey ahead.

He couldn't help but think about the significance of Project Origins. It wasn't just about exploring the cosmos; it was about reconnecting with their roots, understanding where they came from, and honoring the legacy of their ancestors. This mission had the potential to bridge the gap between the past and the present, offering insights that could propel humanity into a new era of knowledge and understanding.

The kettle whistled, snapping him out of his reverie. He poured the hot water over the tea bag and inhaled the calming aroma. As he sipped the tea, he felt a sense of calm wash over him. Tomorrow would be another intense day, but for now, he allowed himself a moment of peace.

The next morning, Dr. Rian arrived at the office even earlier than planned. He wasn't surprised to find Dr. Arius already there, surrounded by data charts and holographic displays.

"Couldn't sleep either, huh?" Rian greeted her with a smile.

Arius looked up, her eyes sparkling with determination. "Nope. Too much is on my mind. Let's get started."

"Now it's time to make an effective plan," said Dr. Arius.

"Do you have any ideas on how to reach their location in this vast universe?" asked Dr. Rian.

Before Arius could respond, the door burst open, and Dr. Klen Dax rushed in, visibly excited.

"Dr. Arius, Dr. Rian, where are you? The signals are being detected again." Dr. Klen exclaimed.

Rian and Arius exchanged a quick glance before hurrying to the communications lab. The room buzzed with activity as scientists clustered around the main console, monitoring the incoming data.

"Show us the latest signals," Dr. Arius instructed, her voice steady but urgent.

Dr. Klen brought up the data on the main screen. "We've been tracking the signals continuously, and they're becoming stronger and more frequent. It's like they're trying to establish consistent contact."

Rian studied the waveform patterns on the display. "Have we pinpointed their origin yet?"

"Not precisely," Klen admitted. "But we've narrowed it down to a specific region in the galaxy. The signals seem to be coming from the Haux star system, around 288 lightyears away."

Arius nodded thoughtfully. "That aligns with some of the data we've decoded from the DNA messages. The coordinates match the location of a possible ancient human outpost."

"Now you should work on their exact location and tell us by 2:00 PM." Ordered Dr. Arius

"Yes ma'am." Said Dr. Klen

"They went back on their original mission along with other members of the team."

"While all the scientists were brainstorming about the possible way of getting to their ancestors,"

"WORMHOLES, yes! It could be a very possible way of shortening our distance and time of travel," exclaimed Dr. Arius.

Dr. Arius's exclamation reverberated through the room, cutting through the intense atmosphere of the brainstorming session like a lightning bolt of inspiration. The mention of wormholes sparked a flurry of excitement among the scientists, igniting a cascade of ideas and possibilities.

"Yeah, it is a great idea," Dr. Rian interjected, his voice measured but tinged with caution, "but it is not a child's play to create or detect a wormhole, and if by any chance there is a mistake, we must have a backup plan."

Dr. Arius nodded in agreement, her gaze focused and determined. "We understand the risks involved, Rian. But this could be our best chance of reaching our ancestors and unlocking the secrets of our past."

Before any further discussion could take place, Dr. Elena entered the room, her expression grave yet determined. "Dr. Arius, Dr. Rian, we have detected the exact origin of the signals. It is a planet in the Haux star system, designated H1009b."

A ripple of excitement swept through the room at the revelation. The prospect of finally pinpointing the source of the mysterious signals filled the scientists with renewed determination.

"Perfect," Dr. Arius declared, her voice ringing with certainty. "Now we know where to go and how to get there. Let's focus our efforts on creating the wormhole."

Dr. Rian nodded in agreement, but his expression remained serious. "Agreed, but we must also develop a backup plan. We can't afford to put all our eggs in one basket, especially when the stakes are this high."

"Of course," Dr. Arius replied, her tone resolute. "But for now, let's focus on one thing at a time. Creating the wormhole is our top priority.

"I have an idea to create a worm hole," said Arius.

"So basically," she began, her tone measured yet enthusiastic, "a wormhole is a type of bend in the space-time fabric. It's like folding a piece of paper so that two distant points touch, allowing for instantaneous travel between them."

As she spoke, Arius paced the room, gesturing animatedly to emphasize her points.

"And here's the key," she continued. "For a wormhole to form, we need to concentrate a massive amount of mass and energy at a single point in space. This creates a gravitational well so deep that it effectively punches through the fabric of spacetime, creating a shortcut between two distant locations."

A murmur of excitement rippled through the room as the scientists processed Arius's explanation. The idea of manipulating spacetime itself to create a wormhole was both daunting and exhilarating.

"So," Arius concluded, her eyes sparkling with determination, "if we concentrate enough mass *and energy at a specific point in space, we could theoretically open up a wormhole that leads to another part of the galaxy. Most likely, the Haux star system, where our ancestors are believed to have originated."*

Her words hung in the air, and the room was filled with a sense of possibility and anticipation. Creating a wormhole was no small feat, but with Arius's idea as a starting point, the scientists felt more optimistic than ever about their chances of unraveling the mysteries of the universe.

Dr. Elena's question hung in the air, prompting a moment of thoughtful silence among the scientists. Dr. Arius pondered for a moment before responding, her expression thoughtful yet determined.

"That's a very good question, Elena," she began, her voice carrying a note of contemplation. "To concentrate such an enormous amount of mass and energy at a single point in space, we'll need to harness the most powerful technologies at our disposal."

Dr. Rian nodded in agreement, his mind already racing with possibilities. "Indeed. We'll need to develop a method of focusing energy with pinpoint precision on a scale that's unprecedented in human history."

Dr. Elena leaned forward, her curiosity palpable. "But how do we achieve that level of precision? And where do we obtain the necessary resources?"

A spark of inspiration flashed in Arius's eyes as she formulated her response. "One possible approach," she began, "is to utilize antimatter. Antimatter possesses the extraordinary ability to release vast amounts of energy when it comes into contact with ordinary matter."

Dr. Lyra's eyes widened with understanding. "So, if we were to develop a highly advanced particle accelerator capable of producing and containing antimatter, we could channel that energy into a focused beam."

"There is no need for that; we have already harnessed the antimatter. The government has control over it; we must ask the government for the antimatter."

Dr. Sarah, the geneticist, interjected with a note of caution. "But creating and controlling antimatter is no easy task. It requires immense precision and safeguards to prevent accidental annihilation."

Dr. Marcus, the historian among them, offered a historical perspective. "Throughout history, humanity has faced seemingly insurmountable challenges and overcome them through ingenuity and perseverance. If we combine our collective knowledge and resources, there's no limit to what we can achieve."

antimatter"

Dr. Arius's announcement was met with a collective sense of relief and anticipation. The idea of utilizing antimatter as a means to concentrate the necessary energy for creating a wormhole seemed to offer a tangible path forward.

Dr. Rian nodded in agreement, his expression reflecting a newfound sense of urgency. "You're right, Arius. The government has access to the antimatter reserves, and it's our responsibility to request access to these resources for the sake of our mission."

Dr. Elena's eyes gleamed with determination as she spoke up. "I'll draft a formal request outlining our intentions and the importance of this endeavor. We'll need to present a compelling case to justify the allocation of such precious resources."

The next day dawned with a sense of anticipation tinged with apprehension as the scientists gathered once again at the research facility. Their minds were abuzz with thoughts of the formal request they had submitted to the government, eager to see if their plea for access to the antimatter reserves had been granted.

As they settled into their seats, Dr. Arius approached the table with a stack of papers in her hands. With a solemn expression, she cleared her throat before speaking.

"Everyone, we have received a formal response from the government regarding our request for

access to the antimatter reserves," she announced, her voice steady despite the undercurrent of tension in the room.

With bated breath, the scientists leaned forward, their eyes fixed on Dr. Arius as she began to read aloud from the letter.

"Dear Dr. Arius Nova and team," she began, "after careful consideration of your proposal and the significance of your mission, we are pleased to inform you that the government has approved your request for access to the antimatter reserves."

A collective sigh of relief swept through the room as the weight of uncertainty lifted from their shoulders. The realization that their ambitious plan was one step closer to becoming a reality filled the scientists with a renewed sense of purpose and determination.

Dr. Elena couldn't suppress a smile as she exchanged triumphant glances with her colleagues. "This is incredible news! We finally have the resources we need to proceed with our mission."

Dr. Rian nodded in agreement, his voice filled with determination. "Now that we have access to the antimatter, it's time to put our plan into action. We must waste no time preparing for the next phase of our journey."

"Very well, now, Dr. Elena, you will be responsible for designing the laser gun and preparing all the necessary files as soon as possible," said Dr. Arius, her tone brisk and authoritative.

Dr. Elena nodded, already envisioning the complex schematics in her mind. "I'll get started immediately. We'll need to ensure that the laser gun is not only powerful enough to generate a wormhole but also stable and controllable."

Dr. Rian chimed in, "We'll also need to coordinate with the engineering team to fabricate the components and assemble the device. This will require precision and expertise across multiple disciplines."

Dr. Marcus added, "Don't worry about that; I'll ensure the safe assembly of all the parts of the laser gun."

With their roles defined, the team dispersed to their respective tasks. Dr. Elena headed straight to her lab, where she began drafting the intricate designs for the laser gun. She worked tirelessly, her mind focused on creating a device capable of harnessing and directing antimatter energy with unprecedented precision.

Meanwhile, Dr. Rian coordinated with various departments, ensuring that all resources were allocated efficiently and timelines were strictly adhered to. He also liaised with government officials to secure the necessary antimatter, emphasizing the importance of their mission.

Dr. Marcus and his team of engineers got to work on fabricating the components. They meticulously followed Dr. Elena's designs, using state-of-the-art technology to craft each piece with exacting precision. Safety protocols were paramount, and Marcus oversaw every detail to ensure the assembly process was flawless.

Dr. Elena's house was a testament to her dual passions for science and art. Located on the outskirts of the city, it was a modern, spacious home with large windows that allowed natural light to flood the rooms, highlighting the sleek lines and elegant decor. Her workspace, a dedicated room at the back of the house, was a perfect blend of functionality and inspiration.

The room was filled with state-of-the-art equipment, including a 3D printer, multiple computer screens, and a large drafting table. The walls were adorned with diagrams of past projects, interspersed with abstract paintings that added a touch of color and creativity. Shelves lined with technical books and journals took up one side of the room, while the other side featured a large window overlooking a serene garden.

It was late evening, and the sun was setting, casting a warm glow over the garden. Dr. Elena sat at her drafting table, her eyes focused on the holographic display in front of her. She was in the zone, her mind buzzing with calculations and design specifications for the laser gun. Soft instrumental music played in the background, providing a soothing counterpoint to the intense concentration required for her work.

Her fingers moved deftly over the holographic controls, adjusting parameters and fine-tuning the design. She paused occasionally to jot down notes in a leather-bound notebook, the pages filled with sketches, formulas, and annotations.

The room was silent except for the occasional hum of the equipment and the gentle rustling of paper.

Taking a break, Elena stretched and walked over to the large window, gazing out at the garden bathed in twilight. The tranquility of the scene contrasted sharply with the high-stakes project she was immersed in. She let out a deep breath, trying to center herself. Her mind wandered briefly to her family and friends, who constantly encouraged her, even though they often worried about her overworking herself.

Returning to her desk, Elena picked up a framed photo of her and her late mentor, Dr. Avery Chen. Dr. Chen had always pushed her to reach beyond the conventional, to explore the uncharted. She could almost hear his voice urging her on, reminding her of the importance of their work.

Setting the photo back, Elena resumed her work with renewed focus. She knew that designing a laser gun powerful enough to create a wormhole was an unprecedented challenge, but the stakes were too high for failure. Every calculation had to be precise, and every component had to be perfectly aligned.

Hours passed unnoticed. The once-vibrant sunset outside had given way to a deep, star-studded night. Elena's eyes flickered with determination as she made the final adjustments to the design. She double-checked the specifications, ensuring the laser gun would harness and direct antimatter energy with the necessary precision.

Suddenly, her communicator buzzed, breaking the silence. It was Dr. Rian checking in on her progress.

"Elena, how's it going?" He asked, his voice tinged with both concern and curiosity.

"Making good progress," she replied, her tone steady. "The designs are almost ready. I just need to finalize a few details."

"Great to hear. Remember, we're all here to support you. Don't hesitate to reach out if you need anything."

"Thanks, Rian. I appreciate it. I'll keep you updated."

As she ended the call, Elena felt a renewed sense of camaraderie. Her colleagues were more than just teammates; they were a family bound by a shared goal. She knew the coming days would be intense, but with their combined efforts, success seemed within reach.

She returned to her designs, working late into the night. The lines between work and home blurred in this quiet sanctuary, where groundbreaking science and personal dedication came together in the quest for discovery. As the hours slipped by, she made the final tweaks to the schematics, her meticulous nature ensuring that no detail was overlooked.

The next morning, the first light of dawn filtered through the window, casting a soft glow over her workspace. Elena stood up, stretching her tired muscles. She glanced at the finished designs on her screen, a sense of accomplishment washing over her. The laser gun was no longer just an idea; it was a detailed plan ready for implementation.

With a deep breath, she sent the final designs to Dr. Rian and Dr. Marcus, along with a detailed report on the specifications and requirements. She knew that this was just the beginning of a long and arduous process, but it was a crucial step forward.

As she prepared a cup of coffee, her thoughts drifted to the mission ahead. Project Origins was more than just a scientific endeavor; it was a journey to rediscover humanity's roots, to connect with their ancestors, and to unlock the mysteries of their past. The potential impact of their work was immense, and the responsibility weighed heavily on her shoulders.

Yet, despite the challenges and uncertainties, Elena felt a sense of purpose. She was part of something greater than herself, a mission that could change the course of history. And with the support of her colleagues and the advancements they were making, she was confident that they could overcome any obstacle in their path.

By mid-morning, the team had convened again, this time in the high-tech laboratory at AWSRA's headquarters. Elena presented her designs, walking them through every detail and explaining how the laser gun would function and how it could be built.

Dr. Marcus was impressed. "These designs are exceptional, Elena. We'll begin fabricating the components immediately. Our team is ready."

Dr. Rian added, "And I've secured the antimatter from the government. Everything is falling into place. We just need to ensure that we follow the plan meticulously."

With a shared sense of excitement and purpose, the team gathered in the high-tech laboratory at AWSRA's headquarters, ready to embark on the next phase of their monumental mission. Dr. Marcus, a seasoned leader with years of experience in engineering and innovation, took the lead, his demeanor a mix of focused determination and quiet confidence.

"We have all the components ready," Marcus announced, his voice echoing in the spacious laboratory. He gestured to the array of materials and equipment spread out before them, each item meticulously organized and labeled. "Let's waste no time and get started on the assembly."

The team members, a diverse group of experts hailing from different corners of the scientific world, were eager to dive into the task at hand. Dr. Elena, with her keen eye for detail and unmatched expertise in laser technology, took charge of monitoring the construction of the laser gun. With precision that bordered on artistry, she ensured that every piece was aligned perfectly according to her meticulously crafted designs.

Meanwhile, Dr. Rian, the consummate coordinator and strategist, seamlessly orchestrated the integration of the antimatter containment system and power supply. His sharp mind and quick thinking were invaluable as he liaised with the engineering team, ensuring that every component was installed with precision and care.

As the hours passed, the laboratory hummed with activity, and the air buzzed with anticipation. The team worked in harmony, their individual skills and talents complementing each other perfectly as they labored tirelessly to bring their vision to life. Despite the challenges they faced, their determination remained unyielding, fueled by the knowledge that they were on the brink of achieving something truly extraordinary.

Finally, after a long day of hard work and unwavering dedication, the final piece fell into place. Dr. Marcus stepped back, his eyes shining with pride as he surveyed their creation. "It's done," he declared, a smile of satisfaction spreading across his face. "Our laser gun is ready."

The rest of the team gathered around, their faces alight with excitement and pride. Dr. Elena ran a thorough diagnostic check, ensuring that every component was functioning flawlessly and meeting the exacting standards set forth in her designs. Dr. Rian meticulously double-checked the safety protocols, leaving no stone unturned in their quest for perfection.

With a nod of approval, Dr. Arius, the visionary leader whose unwavering determination had brought them to this momentous juncture, stepped forward. Her eyes sparkled with excitement as she addressed her colleagues. "Excellent work, everyone. Now, let's prepare for the next phase of our mission. The Haux star system awaits."

After a day filled with exhilarating progress and tireless effort, the team decided to celebrate their success with a well-deserved dinner. Dr. Arius suggested a quaint restaurant not far from AWSRA's headquarters, known for its cozy ambiance and exquisite cuisine. With *unanimous agreement, the team made their way to the restaurant, eager to unwind and revel in each other's company.*

As they settled into their seats around a large table, the atmosphere was filled with a palpable sense of camaraderie and accomplishment. The dim lighting and soft music provided the perfect backdrop for their celebration, casting a warm glow over the room as they exchanged stories and laughter.

Dr. Marcus raised his glass, his eyes twinkling with pride, as he addressed his colleagues. "To our incredible team," he said, his voice filled with genuine admiration, "whose hard work and dedication have brought us to this moment. Here's to the success of our mission and to the countless discoveries that lie ahead."

The team echoed his sentiment, raising their glasses in a toast to their shared achievements. For a moment, the worries and stresses of the day melted away, replaced by a sense of joy and camaraderie that filled the room.

Over the course of the evening, they indulged in delicious food and lively conversation, each moment fostering a deeper sense of connection and unity among them. They shared anecdotes from their past experiences, swapped ideas for the future, and reveled in the sense of possibility that hung in the air.

As the night wore on and the restaurant began to empty out, the team lingered at their table, reluctant to let the evening come to an end. They knew that the challenges ahead would be formidable, but they also knew that they were stronger together, united in their pursuit of knowledge and discovery.

At the break of dawn, the team reconvened at AWSRA's headquarters, their spirits still buoyed by the camaraderie of the previous night's dinner celebration. As the first rays of sunlight streamed through the windows, casting a warm glow over the high-tech facility, the sense of anticipation in the air was palpable.

Dr. Arius, Dr. Rian, Dr. Elena, Dr. Marcus, and the rest of the team gathered in the main conference room, their excitement tempered by a focused determination as they prepared to embark on the next phase of their mission. With their newly constructed laser gun in hand and their plans meticulously laid out, they were *ready to face whatever challenges lay ahead in their quest to unlock the secrets of humanity's ancient past.*

THREE
SPACECRAFT

Good morning, everyone." Dr. Arius greeted them, her voice filled with quiet resolve. "Today marks the beginning of a new chapter in our journey. But before we delve into the mysteries of the cosmos, let's focus on our spacecraft."

Her words were met with nods of agreement from the assembled team. They understood the significance of their spacecraft—the vessel that would carry them across the vast expanse of space to their destination. With their mission parameters set and their goals clear, it was time to ensure that their spacecraft was ready for the challenges that lay ahead.

Dr. Elena stepped forward, her confidence evident, as she began to outline the final preparations for their spacecraft. "Our propulsion systems have undergone rigorous testing," she explained, her voice steady and assured. "We've incorporated the latest advancements in technology to ensure optimal performance and efficiency."

As she spoke, holographic displays flickered to life, showcasing the intricate details of the spacecraft's design. Dr. Elena pointed out key components, detailing their function and importance to the success of their mission.

Dr. Rian listened intently, his mind already racing with thoughts of navigation and trajectory. "What about our course correction systems?" he inquired, his brow furrowed in concentration. "We need to be able to adjust our trajectory as needed to stay on course."

Dr. Elena nodded, acknowledging the importance of precise navigation. "Our course correction systems are state-of-the-art," she replied, her confidence unwavering. "We have redundancies in place to ensure that we can make adjustments as needed to keep us on track."

"Can you please list all the components of the spacecraft?" asked Dr. Arius.

"Certainly," replied Dr. Elena, stepping forward to address Dr. Arius's query. She activated a holographic display, projecting a detailed schematic of the spacecraft onto the table before them.

"As you can see," she began, gesturing toward the display, "our spacecraft is equipped with a comprehensive array of components designed to ensure optimal performance and functionality throughout our journey."

She proceeded to list the components one by one, providing a brief overview of each:

- Propulsion Systems: The heart of our spacecraft consists of advanced engines capable of generating the necessary thrust to propel us through space. These engines have been optimized for efficiency and reliability, allowing us to cover vast distances with minimal fuel consumption.

-

Navigation Systems: Essential for maintaining our course and trajectory, our navigation systems utilize a combination of traditional star charts and cutting-edge computer algorithms to ensure precise positioning at all times. These systems are equipped with redundant backups to mitigate the risk of errors or malfunctions.

Life Support Systems: Vital for sustaining the health and well-being of our crew during the duration of the mission, our life support systems provide a controlled environment within the spacecraft, regulating temperature, air quality, and other essential factors to ensure the comfort and safety of all aboard.

Communication Systems: Facilitating communication between our spacecraft and mission control, our communication systems enable us to maintain contact with Earth throughout our journey. These systems are equipped with encryption protocols and redundancy measures to ensure secure and reliable transmission of data.

Power Systems: Responsible for supplying energy to all onboard systems and equipment, our power systems utilize advanced energy storage technologies to ensure a stable and continuous power supply throughout the mission. These systems are designed to withstand the rigors of deep-space travel and operate efficiently in the harsh conditions of space.

Structural Integrity Systems: Critical for maintaining the structural integrity of our spacecraft, these systems employ advanced materials and design principles to withstand the stresses and strains of space travel. Rigorous testing and quality control measures ensure that our spacecraft is robust and resilient against the rigors of the journey.

Payload Systems: Housing our scientific instruments, equipment, and supplies, our payload systems are designed to maximize space utilization while ensuring easy access and retrieval of essential items. These systems are modular and adaptable, allowing us to customize our payload according to the specific requirements of our mission.

As Dr. Elena concluded her overview, she looked to Dr. Arius, awaiting any further questions or clarifications. The team members studied the holographic display intently, their minds already racing with thoughts of the challenges and discoveries that lay ahead in their journey to the Haux star system.

"Thank you very much, Dr. Elena, Now our goal is to create all these components separately and assemble them; it would be easy and efficient for us." Said Dr. Arius.

"Let's begin with the propulsion system," Dr. Marcus announced, taking charge of the next phase of their mission. "This is the cornerstone of our spacecraft, and its efficiency will determine our ability to reach our destination."

The team members gathered around him, their attention focused as he outlined the intricate details of the propulsion system design. Dr. Elena nodded in agreement, already visualizing the components and their interactions within the spacecraft.

"We'll need to ensure that the propulsion system is not only powerful but also reliable," Dr. Marcus continued, his voice steady and assured. "We can't afford any malfunctions or delays once we're on our way to the Haux star system."

Dr. Rian nodded in agreement, his mind already racing with thoughts of trajectory and navigation. "What about fuel efficiency?" he inquired, his brow furrowed in concentration. "We need to make sure that we have enough fuel to sustain our journey without weighing down the spacecraft."

Dr. Marcus nodded in acknowledgment of the valid concern. "Fuel efficiency is indeed crucial," he agreed. "That's why we've incorporated advanced propulsion technologies that maximize thrust while minimizing fuel consumption. With proper planning and management, we should have more than enough fuel to reach our destination."

With a shared understanding of their goals, the team members set to work, each contributing their expertise to the fabrication of the propulsion system. Dr. Marcus supervised the assembly process with meticulous attention to detail, ensuring that each component was crafted to the highest standards of quality and precision.

The team's determination burned bright as they focused solely on the propulsion system, pushing themselves to the limit to complete it in record time. With every member working in perfect harmony, the assembly process progressed smoothly, with each component slotting into place with precision and purpose.

Dr. Marcus led the charge with unwavering dedication, his expertise guiding the team through every step of the assembly process. His steady hand and keen eye ensured that each connection was secure and that each component aligned perfectly as the propulsion system took shape before their eyes.

Dr. Elena and her team of engineers worked tirelessly alongside him, their fingers flying over control panels and monitors as they monitored the progress of the assembly. They adjusted parameters, fine-tuned systems, and performed countless tests to ensure that every aspect of the propulsion system met their exacting standards.

As the hours passed and fatigue threatened to set in, the team's determination only grew stronger. They pushed through exhaustion, fueled by the knowledge that their efforts were bringing them one step closer to their ultimate goal—the Haux star system and the mysteries it held.

Finally, as the clock struck midnight, the last bolt was tightened, the final circuit connected, and the propulsion system stood complete before them. Dr. Marcus stepped back, a sense of pride swelling within him as he surveyed their handiwork. "It's done," he declared, a smile of satisfaction spreading across his face. "Our propulsion system is ready."

The rest of the team gathered around, their exhaustion momentarily forgotten in the face of their accomplishment. They exchanged smiles and nods of agreement, their spirits buoyed by the knowledge that they had achieved something truly remarkable.

As they prepared to leave the laboratory and rest after a long night of hard work, they knew that their journey was far from over. But with the propulsion system now complete, they were one step closer to unlocking the secrets of the cosmos and uncovering the truth about humanity's ancient past.

Amidst the meticulous planning and intense preparation for their mission, a seemingly minor yet potentially significant issue emerged, causing a momentary pause in the team's progress.

During a routine systems check, Dr. Elena noticed a discrepancy in the alignment of one of the propulsion system's thrusters. It was a small deviation, barely perceptible to the untrained eye, but it had the potential to compromise the spacecraft's trajectory if left unaddressed.

Gathering the team in the main conference room, Dr. Elena presented her findings with a sense of urgency. "We've encountered a small hiccup in the propulsion system," she explained, projecting the relevant data onto the holographic display for all to see. "One of the thrusters appears to be misaligned by a fraction of a degree."

Dr. Marcus furrowed his brow in thought as he examined the data, his mind already racing through possible solutions. "It's a minor issue, but we can't afford to overlook it," he remarked, his tone serious yet composed.

Dr. Arius nodded in agreement, her expression thoughtful. "We need to address this immediately to ensure that our trajectory remains on course," she said, her voice carrying a note of determination.

With the problem identified, the team wasted no time in springing into action. Dr. Elena and her team of engineers set to work, carefully recalibrating the thruster to correct the misalignment. It was a delicate process, requiring precision and attention to detail, but they approached the task with unwavering focus and determination.

As the hours passed, the team worked tirelessly, their efforts fueled by the knowledge that even the smallest detail could have significant consequences in the vast expanse of space. And when the thruster was finally realigned to perfection, a sense of relief washed over them, tempered by the realization that their vigilance and dedication had ensured the success of their mission.

With the issue resolved and their trajectory back on track, the team returned to their preparations with renewed focus and determination. They knew that in the unforgiving void of space, even the smallest problems could have monumental implications, and they were determined to face whatever challenges lay ahead with courage and resilience.

With the minor issue of the thruster alignment resolved, the team wasted no time in continuing their progress. The next day dawned with a renewed sense of purpose as they set their sights on fabricating three more crucial components for the spacecraft.

Dr. Elena, leading the charge once again, rallied her team of engineers as they delved into the intricate details of their designs. With precision and expertise, they began the meticulous process of crafting each component, ensuring that every piece met the exacting standards required for space travel.

Meanwhile, Dr. Marcus and his team of engineers focused on the construction of the spacecraft's navigation system. Drawing on their years of experience and expertise, they worked tirelessly to assemble the intricate network of sensors and control modules that would guide the spacecraft safely through the depths of space.

At the same time, Dr. Rian coordinated with suppliers and logistics teams to ensure that all necessary materials and resources were readily available. His keen eye for detail and knack for organization proved invaluable as he navigated the complex web of supply chains and procurement processes.

As the day wore on and the sun dipped below the horizon, the team's efforts bore fruit as three more components were completed and integrated seamlessly into the spacecraft's framework. With each success, their confidence grew, fueling their determination to overcome any obstacle that stood in their way.

And as they gathered once again in the main conference room to review their progress, a sense of pride washed over them. They were a team united in purpose, driven by a shared vision of exploration and discovery. And with each passing day, they drew one step closer to realizing their dreams of unlocking the secrets of the universe.

As the first rays of dawn painted the sky in hues of orange and gold, a sense of anticipation hung thick in the air at AWSRA's headquarters. The team had worked tirelessly through the night, fueled by determination and a shared sense of purpose, and now their efforts were about to bear fruit in the most spectacular way imaginable.

With bated breath and eager hearts, the team gathered in the main hangar, their eyes fixed on the imposing silhouette of the spacecraft before them. It stood like a sentinel, a beacon of hope and possibility in the vast expanse of the hangar; its sleek lines and gleaming surfaces were a testament to the ingenuity and dedication of those who had brought it to life.

Dr. Arius, her voice filled with quiet reverence, addressed her colleagues with a sense of awe and wonder. "Today, my friends, marks the dawn of a new era in human exploration," she began, her words ringing out with a sense of solemnity and purpose. "For too long, we have gazed up at the stars and wondered what secrets they hold. Today, we take the first step towards unlocking those secrets, towards charting a course through the cosmos and uncovering the mysteries that lie beyond."

Dr. Rian, his eyes sparkling with excitement, nodded in agreement. "Indeed, Arius," he replied, his voice tinged with anticipation. "Today, we stand on the brink of history, on the cusp of a journey that will take us to the very edges of the universe and back again. And as we prepare to embark on this grand adventure, let us remember the countless hours of toil and sacrifice that have brought us to this moment, and let us carry forward the spirit of exploration and discovery that has always defined our species."

With a sense of reverence and determination, the team gathered around the spacecraft, their hands reaching out to touch its smooth surfaces, their hearts filled with a sense of wonder and excitement. They knew that they were about to embark on a journey unlike any other, a journey that would push the boundaries of human knowledge and understanding and forever change the course of history.

Meanwhile, as the team marveled at the spacecraft, Dr. Arius stepped forward, her eyes gleaming with determination. "But our work is not yet complete," she declared, her voice ringing out with authority. "We must ensure that our spacecraft is equipped to face whatever challenges lie ahead. And to that end, I have instructed that the laser gun be installed without delay."

With a sense of purpose, the team sprang into action, their movements swift and coordinated as they prepared to integrate the powerful weapon into the spacecraft's arsenal. Dr. Elena and her team of engineers worked tirelessly, carefully aligning the laser gun with the spacecraft's framework and ensuring that it was securely fastened in place.

Dr. Marcus and his team, meanwhile, focused on the intricate task of linking the laser gun to the spacecraft's systems, ensuring seamless integration and optimal performance. Their expertise and attention to detail were evident as they worked, their hands moving with practiced precision as they connected wires and calibrated controls.

And as the final bolts were tightened and the last connections made, a sense of satisfaction washed over the team. The laser gun, gleaming with power and potential, now stood ready to defend the spacecraft against any threats that might arise during its journey through the depths of space.

Dr. Arius nodded in approval as she surveyed their handiwork, her expression one of quiet satisfaction. "Well done, everyone," she remarked, her voice filled with pride. "With the laser gun installed, our spacecraft is now truly ready to embark on its historic journey. Let us proceed with confidence, knowing that we have equipped ourselves to face whatever challenges may come our way."

"And with those words, the team gathered once more around the spacecraft, their hearts filled with anticipation and excitement. They knew that they were on the brink of something truly extraordinary, something that would push the boundaries of human knowledge and redefine the possibilities of space exploration. And as they prepared to launch into the unknown, they did so with a sense of purpose and determination, ready to embrace whatever wonders and dangers awaited them among the stars."

"What about our backup plan?" Asked Dr. Rian

Dr. Rian's question hung in the air, a reminder of the importance of contingency planning in the face of uncertainty. Dr. Arius nodded thoughtfully, acknowledging the validity of his concern.

"You're right, Rian," she replied, her voice tinged with solemnity. "While our focus has been on ensuring the success of our primary mission, we cannot afford to overlook the need for a backup plan. The journey ahead is fraught with unknowns, and it is our responsibility to be prepared for any eventuality."

Turning to face the team, Dr. Arius continued, her gaze steady and unwavering. "I propose that we designate a portion of our resources and manpower to developing a comprehensive backup plan. This plan should outline alternative strategies and contingencies to address potential challenges or setbacks that may arise during our mission."

Dr. Elena, ever the pragmatist, spoke up, her tone measured yet decisive. "I agree, Arius. It would be prudent for us to identify potential risks and vulnerabilities and devise strategies to mitigate them. This will ensure that we are not caught off guard and that we have a plan in place to adapt and overcome any obstacles we may encounter."

The rest of the team nodded in agreement, their expressions reflecting a shared commitment to ensuring the success and safety of their mission. With Dr. Arius's guidance, they set to work, brainstorming ideas and drafting plans for various scenarios, from technical malfunctions to unforeseen encounters with extraterrestrial phenomena.

Hours passed in a blur as the team delved deeper into their preparations, their determination unyielding in the face of uncertainty. By the time they adjourned for the day, they had outlined a comprehensive backup plan, complete with protocols and procedures to address a wide range of potential challenges.

"As they left the meeting room, a sense of reassurance washed over the team, knowing that they had taken proactive steps to safeguard their mission and ensure its success. For in the vast expanse of space, where the unknown lurked around every corner, preparation was the key to survival. And with their backup plan in place, they were ready to face whatever the universe had in store."

FOUR
LAUNCH!

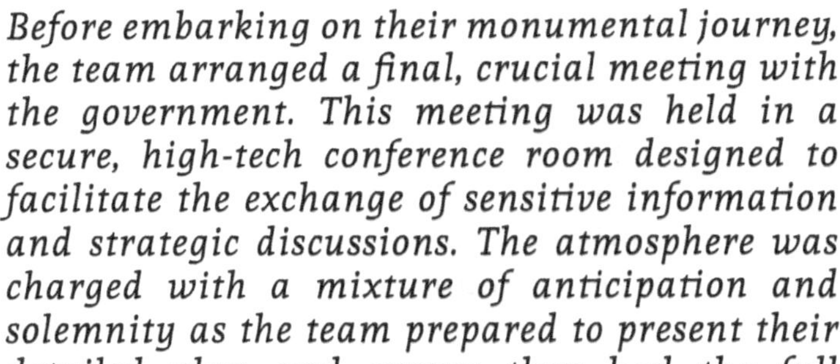

Before embarking on their monumental journey, the team arranged a final, crucial meeting with the government. This meeting was held in a secure, high-tech conference room designed to facilitate the exchange of sensitive information and strategic discussions. The atmosphere was charged with a mixture of anticipation and solemnity as the team prepared to present their detailed plan and ensure they had the full backing and resources needed for their mission.

Dr. Arius began the presentation, her voice steady and confident as she outlined their ambitious plan. "Our mission is to depart Earth and navigate to a precise location near Neptune, where the gravitational forces are minimal and ideal for our operation," she explained. "At this juncture, we will use our advanced laser gun to concentrate mass and energy, creating a wormhole."

Dr. Rian continued, detailing the technical aspects and the rigorous safety protocols they had established. "Creating a wormhole is a complex and delicate process, but we have ensured every precaution is in place. Our laser gun, which doubles as a defensive tool, is equipped with antimatter harnessed under strict control."

The officials listened intently as Dr. Elena elaborated on the journey through the wormhole. "Once the wormhole is stabilized, we will traverse through it to the Haux star system. Our destination is the planet H1009b, from which we have detected faint signals. Upon arrival, our primary objective is to establish contact with any potential inhabitants. If direct communication is not feasible, we will conduct an extensive exploration of the planet to gather information."

Dr. Marcus addressed the logistical and engineering challenges. "Our spacecraft is equipped with state-of-the-art technology to ensure safe travel and successful completion of our mission. The laser gun is securely integrated, and all systems have been rigorously tested."

The government officials asked several probing questions, particularly about the backup plan. Dr. Arius reassured them, "In the event of any unforeseen complications, we have a secondary plan in place. We can return through the wormhole or utilize alternative communication methods to request assistance."

After thorough deliberation, the officials gave their approval, recognizing the potential scientific breakthroughs and the historical significance of the mission. With the government's endorsement and resources secured, the team left the meeting with renewed determination and a clear mandate.

This final meeting solidified their resolve and provided the necessary support for their unprecedented journey. As they prepared to leave Earth, the weight of their mission and the potential discoveries that awaited them filled them with a sense of purpose and excitement.

The next chapter of their adventure was about to begin, promising to push the boundaries of human knowledge and exploration.

"Their launch was planned two days later."

"Their launch was planned for two days later," Dr. Arius announced as the team exited the government meeting room. With the final endorsement secured, the countdown to their historic journey had begun.

The next forty-eight hours were a whirlwind of activity. Every team member was laser-focused on final preparations, ensuring that no detail was overlooked. In the high-tech laboratory at AWSRA's headquarters, engineers and scientists worked tirelessly to double-check all systems, conduct last-minute tests, and finalize the integration of the laser gun.

Dr. Elena spent her time running diagnostics on the propulsion system and making sure the antimatter containment was flawless. She was often seen with a determined look on her face, a tablet in hand, constantly analyzing data and making minute adjustments.

Dr. Rian coordinated with logistics to ensure all supplies were onboard and properly stowed. He held briefings with the crew to review emergency protocols, ensuring everyone knew their roles and responsibilities in various scenarios. He also liaised with mission control to establish communication protocols for the journey and the subsequent exploration of H1009b.

Dr. Marcus supervised the final assembly checks, paying close attention to the installation of the laser gun. He and his team of engineers meticulously ensured that every bolt was secure, every connection was stable, and all systems were fully operational. Safety protocols were reviewed and reinforced to guarantee that the crew could handle any technical difficulties that might arise during the mission.

The atmosphere was a mix of nervous energy and palpable excitement. The enormity of what they were about to undertake weighed heavily on everyone's minds, but it also fueled their determination. They were not just leaving Earth; they were pushing the boundaries of human knowledge and venturing into the unknown.

The night before the launch, the team gathered for a final review of their plan. Dr. Arius stood at the front of the room, her expression one of quiet resolve. "Tomorrow, we embark on a journey that will take us to the very edges of the universe and beyond. Our primary objective is to reach the Haux star system, open a wormhole, and explore the planet H1009b. This is our chance to uncover the secrets of our ancestors and expand our understanding of the cosmos."

On the day of the launch, Dr. Sarah Dax joined the rest of the team at AWSRA's headquarters, her presence having a steady influence. As the spacecraft stood ready on the launchpad, she offered final words of encouragement and wisdom. "Remember, our journey is as much about exploration as it is about understanding our place in the universe. We are not just traveling through space; we are delving into the very fabric of reality itself.

With everything in place, the team disbanded for a few hours of rest, knowing that the following day would mark the beginning of an extraordinary chapter in human history.

As dawn broke on the day of the launch, the spacecraft stood ready on the launchpad, a testament to their hard work and determination. The crew, clad in their space suits, made their final preparations. Hearts pounding with anticipation, they boarded the spacecraft and took their positions.

Dr. Arius's voice crackled over the intercom, filled with a mixture of excitement and resolve. "Mission control, this is AWSRA-1. We are ready for launch."

The countdown began, and with each passing second, the reality of their journey became more tangible. At the final moment, the engines roared to life, and the spacecraft lifted off, ascending towards the stars. The journey to the Haux star system had begun, and with it, the promise of unlocking the mysteries of the universe.

As the sun dipped below the horizon, casting long shadows across the AWSRA headquarters, the team gathered in the mission control room, their faces illuminated by the glow of countless monitors and control panels. The air was thick with a blend of excitement, nerves, and a palpable sense of history in the making. This was it—the culmination of months of tireless work and unwavering dedication. The countdown to launch had begun.

"Ten minutes to launch," announced the voice over the intercom, clear and steady despite the undercurrent of tension that ran through the room.

Dr. Arius, standing at the forefront, took a deep breath and turned to address the team. "We've done everything we can to prepare for this moment. Our mission is clear: to travel to the edge of Neptune's gravitational field, create a wormhole, and journey to the Haux star system. We're ready."

Dr. Rian nodded, his usual calm demeanor now tinged with a rare spark of excitement. "All systems are good to go. Propulsion is green, life support is stable, and our trajectory is locked in."

Dr. Elena, her eyes reflecting the light of her monitors, confirmed, "The laser gun is fully integrated and operational. We're ready to create that wormhole as soon as we reach our target position."

Dr. Marcus and his team had done their part with meticulous precision. "The spacecraft is in top condition," Marcus assured. "We've triple-checked every component. We're ready for anything."

Dr. Sarah Dax added a final note of caution and preparedness. "All biological containment protocols are in place. Should we encounter any alien life forms, we're fully equipped to handle the situation safely. Let's remember, this isn't just a mission of exploration—it's a mission of protection, both for ourselves and whatever we might find."

As the clock ticked down, the team members took their positions. Each knew their role and the importance of their actions in the critical moments ahead.

"Five minutes to launch," the intercom announced.

The tension in the room was palpable, yet there was an undercurrent of calm, a quiet confidence born of countless hours of preparation and unwavering dedication to their mission.

"Two minutes to launch."

Dr. Arius took a final look around, her gaze lingering on each member of her team. "Whatever happens out there, know that we've made history just by reaching this point. Let's make our mark on the stars."

"One minute to launch. Commence the final system check."

One by one, the team members confirmed their readiness. "Life support systems: check. Propulsion systems: check. Navigation systems: check. Laser gun systems: check. Communication systems: check."

"Thirty seconds to launch."

The countdown continued, with each second bringing them closer to the unknown.

"Ten, nine, eight, seven, six, five, four, three, two, one... ignition."

With a deafening roar, the spacecraft's engines sprang to life, and the vessel began its ascent, lifting off the ground and rising into the night sky. The mission control room erupted in applause and cheers, but there was no time for celebration yet—the real journey was just beginning.

As the spacecraft climbed higher and higher, leaving Earth behind, the team inside remained focused and resolute. Their destination is the edge of Neptune's gravitational field. Their goal is to create a wormhole and venture into the Haux star system. Their mission is to unlock the secrets of the cosmos and perhaps find the link to their ancestors.

"Woah, we did it!" exclaimed Dr. Arius.

"Yes!" said Dr. Marcus.

As the spacecraft reached the outer orbit of Earth, a sense of anticipation filled the cabin. Dr. Arius Nova, the lead scientist, stood at the control panel, her eyes fixed on the vast expanse of space beyond.

"We've reached the outer orbit of the earth," she announced, her voice tinged with excitement. "Next stop, the border of Neptune's gravitational influence."

Dr. Lyra Nova, the historian, glanced out of the viewport, her breath catching at the sight of Earth suspended in the darkness of space. "It's a remarkable sight," she murmured, her voice barely above a whisper. "To think that we're leaving our home behind to explore the unknown."

Dr. Sarah Dax, the geneticist, busied herself with her instruments, analyzing the data streaming in from their sensors. "We need to remain vigilant," she reminded her colleagues. "Even in the emptiness of space, there are dangers we must be prepared for."

Dr. Rian Dax, the project coordinator, nodded in agreement, his gaze fixed on the control panel. "Indeed," he replied. "But with our combined expertise and determination, I have every confidence that we will succeed in our mission."

Dr. Marcus Dax, the archaeologist, looked out into the darkness of space, his mind filled with *wonder at the mysteries that lay ahead. "It's a privilege to be a part of this journey," he said quietly. "To have the opportunity to uncover the secrets of the cosmos."*

Dr. Elena Nova, the propulsion engineer, guided the spacecraft with practiced precision, her hands moving deftly across the controls. "We're on course," she confirmed. "And with each passing moment, we're one step closer to our destination."

As the spacecraft continued on its journey, the team members settled into their roles, their minds focused on the task at hand. They knew that the challenges they would face in the days ahead would test their strength, their courage, and their resolve. But they were determined to press forward, driven by the promise of discovery and the hope of a brighter future for humanity.

FIVE

V'RETH

As the spacecraft approached the outer reaches of Mars's orbit, the crew members gathered around the main viewscreen, their anticipation palpable in the confined space of the command deck. Dr. Arius Nova, the mission leader, stood at the forefront, her gaze fixed on the vast expanse of space ahead. "We're nearing the outer edges of Mars's orbit," she announced, her voice echoing with a sense of urgency. "Prepare for any potential anomalies or obstacles."

Dr. Rian Dax, the astrophysics expert, furrowed his brow as he analyzed the incoming data streams. "Keep an eye on the gravitational fluctuations," he advised, his tone measured yet alert. "We're entering a region where the gravitational pull of Mars could affect our trajectory."

Dr. Sarah Ahmed, the geneticist, glanced up from her console, her attention momentarily diverted from her research. "I'm detecting unusual energy readings," she reported, her voice tinged with concern. "It could be interference from the nearby asteroid belt. We should proceed with caution."

Dr. Marcus Chang, the archaeologist, leaned forward in his seat, his eyes scanning the viewscreen for any signs of activity. "Be on the lookout for debris or meteoroids," he warned, his voice steady despite the underlying tension. "We don't want any surprises at this stage of the mission."

Dr. Elena Garcia, the propulsion engineer, monitored the spacecraft's thruster systems with meticulous attention to detail. "Thruster output is stable," she confirmed, her voice crisp and authoritative. "We should be able to navigate through this region without any major issues."

Dr. Lyra Nova, the historian, observed the scene with a mixture of awe and trepidation. "This is a critical moment in our journey," she remarked, her voice reflective. "We're venturing into uncharted territory, pushing the boundaries of human exploration."

As the spacecraft continued on its course, the crew members remained vigilant, their focus unwavering as they braced themselves for whatever challenges lay ahead in the depths of space.

As the spacecraft ventured deeper into the outer reaches of Mars's orbit, a sudden alarm pierced the air of the command deck. Dr. Elena Garcia's brow furrowed as she quickly assessed the situation, her eyes fixed on the control panel displaying the status of the thruster systems.

"We've got a problem," Dr. Elena announced, her voice laced with urgency. "One of the thrusters has been deactivated. It's showing signs of overheating."

Dr. Marcus Dax leaned in closer to inspect the data readouts, his expression grave. "It's not completely gone, but it's definitely compromised," he confirmed, his voice steady despite the tension in the air. "We need to act fast before it causes further damage."

Dr. Arius Nova, the mission leader, wasted no time in issuing orders. "Initiate emergency protocols," she commanded, her voice cutting through the chaos with authority. "We need to stabilize the thruster and prevent any potential cascading failures."

Dr. Rian Dax, the astrophysics expert, sprang into action, his fingers flying across the control panel as he rerouted power to the remaining thrusters. "Compensate for the loss of thrust," he directed, his voice calm and focused. "We need to maintain our trajectory while we assess the extent of the damage."

Dr. Sarah Dax, the geneticist, monitored the spacecraft's vital signs with a sense of urgency, her eyes darting between the various readouts. "Keep an eye on the structural integrity," she advised, her voice tinged with concern. "We don't want any hull breaches or internal damage."

Dr. Lyra Nova, the historian, offered words of encouragement to her fellow crew members, her voice a reassuring presence amidst the tension. "Stay calm and focused," she urged, her tone steady and unwavering. "We've faced challenges before, and we'll overcome this one together."

Dr. Marcus Dax, the engineering lead, proposed a novel approach to cool down the overheated thruster using a combination of specialized coolant and automated thermal regulation systems. His idea was met with nods of approval from the rest of the team, who recognized the urgency of the situation.

Dr. Elena Nova, renowned for her ingenuity in propulsion systems, devised a temporary workaround to redistribute the remaining thrust among the functioning thrusters, ensuring that the spacecraft could maintain its course without overtaxing the compromised unit.

Dr. Rian Dax, the mission coordinator, coordinated with ground control to download software patches and diagnostic tools that could help diagnose the root cause of the thruster malfunction and implement corrective measures remotely.

Dr. Lyra Nova, the historian, drew inspiration from historical accounts of space exploration and crisis management, offering strategic guidance and moral support to her colleagues as they worked tirelessly to resolve the problem.

"With each member of the team contributing their unique skills and perspectives, they implemented a series of innovative solutions that gradually stabilized the thruster and restored its functionality. As the spacecraft continued on its journey, the crew breathed a collective sigh of relief, knowing that they had overcome yet another obstacle through collaboration and ingenuity."

After successfully resolving the issue with the thruster, the team breathed a collective sigh of relief, and the tension that had gripped them slowly dissipated. With the immediate crisis averted, Dr. Arius Nova, the leader of the expedition, instructed everyone to take some much-needed rest.

Dr. Elena Garcia, feeling a wave of exhaustion wash over her after the intense troubleshooting session, gratefully retreated to her quarters. Dr. Marcus Chang, satisfied with the outcome but still vigilant, ensured that the spacecraft's systems were stable before allowing himself a moment of respite.

Dr. Rian Dax, ever the vigilant coordinator, remained in the command center for a while longer, monitoring the spacecraft's vital signs and liaising with ground control to provide status updates. Dr. Sarah Ahmed and Dr. Lyra Nova, their minds still buzzing with adrenaline, exchanged a few words of encouragement before retiring to their respective quarters.

As the crew settled into their sleeping quarters, the hum of the spacecraft's systems providing a soothing backdrop, they allowed themselves to relax, if only for a moment. The weight of their monumental task still hung heavy in the air, but for now, they were content to bask in the quiet stillness of space, knowing that they had faced adversity and emerged stronger for it.

After resolving the issue with the overheated thruster near Mars' orbit, the crew took some much-needed rest. They floated in the zero-gravity sleeping quarters, their minds temporarily freed from the weight of their mission.

Hours later, as the spacecraft continued its silent voyage through the cosmos, the crew began to stir. The gentle hum of the ship's systems served as a comforting reminder of their progress.

Dr. Arius Nova was the first to awaken. She stretched and took a deep breath, feeling the excitement of their journey wash over her again. One by one, the rest of the crew emerged from their sleeping quarters.

Dr. Elena Nova, her mind always abuzz with ideas, floated over to the control panels to check the ship's status. "All systems are green," she reported with a smile.

Dr. Marcus Dax joined her, his eyes scanning the readouts. "That thruster's temperature is back within safe limits. We should be good to go."

Dr. Rian Dax gathered the team in the common area. "Alright, team, let's discuss our next steps. We're past Mars and heading towards the outer orbit, where we'll create the wormhole."

Dr. Sarah Dax, their biologist and geneticist, floated in with a serene expression. "I've been thinking about the implications of what we might find on H1009b. The possibilities for genetic discoveries are endless."

Dr. Lyra Nova, her eyes bright with excitement, added, "And the technological advancements we could achieve from understanding their signals. This is groundbreaking."

Arius nodded. "Absolutely. But first, let's make sure everything is ready for the wormhole creation. Marcus, how's the laser gun integration?"

"Solid," Marcus replied. "The system is stable and ready for deployment. We just need to make sure everything else is in sync when we fire it up."

Elena chimed in, "I'll double-check the power systems and make sure we have enough energy reserves."

As they continued their casual discussion, a sense of camaraderie and shared purpose filled the room. They talked about their hopes, the potential discoveries, and even shared a few laughs about the quirks of living in space.

Suddenly, a light on the control panel blinks. Elena floated over to check it out. "It's just a proximity alert. We're nearing the outer edge of

Mars' orbit. Everything's on track."

Arius smiled. "Alright, team, let's get ready for the next phase. We've got a wormhole to create and a star system to explore."

With that, the crew felt a renewed sense of purpose. They were ready to face the unknown, armed with their expertise, determination, and the bond they had forged on this extraordinary journey.

Dr. Arius Nova, their leader, floated over to the main control panel. "We're nearing our destination," she announced. "Get ready, everyone. This is where the real work begins."

The crew members responded with a mixture of excitement and focus. They had rehearsed this moment countless times, but now it was real. Each of them had a crucial role to play in the success of their mission.

Dr. Elena Garcia monitored the ship's navigation systems, ensuring they stayed on course. "We're almost there," she confirmed. "Just a few more adjustments."

Dr. Marcus Chang, their engineering genius, was in the engine room, making final checks on the propulsion systems and the laser gun. "Everything looks good here. The thrusters are stable, and the laser gun is primed and ready."

Dr. Rian Dax joined him, overseeing the antimatter containment system. "The antimatter is secure. We have enough power to create the wormhole and sustain it for the necessary duration."

Dr. Sarah Ahmed, their biologist and geneticist, floated in the common area, preparing the data collection systems. "I've set up all the necessary protocols for when we reach H1009b. We'll be ready to gather any biological and environmental data we come across."

Dr. Lyra Nova, the technology specialist, was in the communications room, ready to decode any signals and establish communication with potential alien life. "I'm ready to intercept and analyze any transmissions. If there's anything out there, we'll find it."

As they approached the designated point, a sense of unity and purpose settled over the team. They had trained for this, and now they were on the cusp of a historic moment.

"Alright, everyone," Arius called out, her voice steady and calm. "We're in position. Marcus, prepare to fire the laser gun."

Marcus's voice came through the intercom. "Roger that. Initiating final checks."

Elena's fingers flew over the controls, ensuring that all systems were aligned. "All systems are green. We're good to go."

Arius took a deep breath, her eyes meeting those of her team members. "Let's make history. Fire the laser gun."

Marcus activated the laser gun, and a beam of concentrated energy shot out into the void of space, aimed precisely at the coordinates they had calculated. Just as the beam was about to reach its target, an alarm blared through the spacecraft.

"Incoming object!" Lyra's voice rang out urgently. "Something's approaching us fast."

The crew's attention shifted to the external monitors. A sleek, unfamiliar spacecraft was rapidly closing in on them. It was unlike any design they had ever seen; its surface was smooth and metallic, reflecting the distant starlight.

"Everyone, stay alert," Arius commanded. "Prepare for potential contact."

The alien ship came to a stop a short distance from their own, hovering silently. After a tense moment, a communication signal flashed on Lyra's console. "They're trying to communicate with us," she said.

"Open a channel," Arius instructed.

The viewscreen flickered to life, revealing an alien being. Its appearance was humanoid but distinctly otherworldly, with luminous skin and large, expressive eyes. The alien spoke in a series of melodic tones that Lyra's systems quickly translated.

"Greetings, travelers," the alien said. "We are the V'reth. We have been observing your journey and your preparations to create a wormhole. We demand that you cease your activities immediately and surrender."

The crew exchanged astonished glances. "Surrender?" Arius asked, regaining her composure. "Why would we do that?"

The V'reth being's expression hardened, and its tone grew menacing. "Your technology is a threat to our existence. You will comply or face the consequences."

Dr. Rian stepped forward, his skepticism evident. "How can we trust you?"

The alien's eyes met his, radiating hostility. "Trust is irrelevant. You have no choice."

Arius considered this, then shook her head. "We can't surrender. Our mission is too important."

The V'reth's expression turned icy. "Then you have chosen destruction."

With a swift motion, the alien ship fired a beam of energy at the AWSRA spacecraft. The ship shuddered under the impact, alarms blaring as systems went into overdrive to compensate.

"Return fire!" Arius commanded. "Marcus, use the laser gun!"

Marcus's hands flew over the controls, and the laser gun roared to life, sending a beam of energy back at the alien ship. The two vessels exchanged fire, the void of space lighting up with the intensity of their battle.

Elena struggled to maintain control of the ship's navigation, her face a mask of concentration. "We're taking heavy damage! We need to find a way to escape!"

Rian's voice cut through the chaos. "If we can reach the wormhole coordinates, we might be able to lose them!"

Arius nodded, her expression grim. "Elena, plot a course for the wormhole. Marcus, keep firing. We need to buy some time."

With the alien ship hot on their heels, the crew of the AWSRA spacecraft fought with everything they had. The battle was fierce, but their determination was unyielding. As they neared the coordinates for the wormhole, a sense of urgency drove them forward.

"Hold on!" Elena shouted. "Initiating the wormhole creation sequence!"

The ship's systems surged with power as the laser gun fired one last, concentrated beam. The fabric of space-time began to warp and twist, forming a shimmering portal ahead of them.

"We're almost there!" Rian yelled. "Just a little further!"

With a final burst of speed, the AWSRA spacecraft plunged into the wormhole, the alien ship's fire trailing behind them. The view outside the windows shifted, the familiar stars replaced by swirling lights and colors as they traveled through the bridge in space-time.

Their journey to the Haux star system had begun, and with it came the promise of new discoveries and unimaginable possibilities. The team was ready to face whatever lay ahead, united in their mission, and driven by the quest for knowledge.

As the wormhole stabilized, a sudden jolt ran through the ship. Marcus's voice crackled over the intercom. "One of the thrusters has overheated! We need to shut it down before it causes more damage."

Arius's voice was calm but urgent. "Do it. We can't afford to lose propulsion now."

Marcus deactivated the thruster, and the ship's speed adjusted slightly. "It's not completely gone, just overheated. We can repair it once we're through the wormhole."

"They emerged on the other side, and the vast expanse of the Haux star system spread out before them. The alien ship, damaged but not destroyed, appeared to follow them, maintaining a wary distance."

"It looks like we bought ourselves some time," Lyra said, her eyes on the monitors. "But they're still on our tail."

Arius nodded. "Let's use this time to repair the thruster and get ready for whatever comes next. We need to stay ahead of them."

The crew sprang into action, their movements swift and coordinated. Dr. Sarah Ahmed monitored the ship's systems, ensuring that the environmental controls were stable. Dr. Elena and Dr. Marcus worked on the thruster; their expertise and precision were evident as they made the necessary repairs.

SIX

INTERACTION

After the repairs were completed, the crew gathered on the observation deck to witness the breathtaking sights of the Haux star system. As they looked out through the reinforced windows, they were greeted by a panorama of swirling nebulas, distant star clusters, and the brilliant glow of the Haux star itself.

"Wow, this is incredible," Lyra breathed, her eyes wide with wonder as she took in the mesmerizing views.

Arius nodded in agreement, a smile playing at the corners of her lips. "It's even more beautiful than I imagined. This is why we do what we do."

Dr. Sarah, her gaze fixed on the distant stars, felt a sense of awe wash over her. "To think that we're the first humans to lay eyes on this... It's humbling."

Dr. Marcus, ever the pragmatist, couldn't help but marvel at the scientific implications of their discovery. "Imagine what we could learn from studying these celestial phenomena up close. It's a goldmine of data."

Rian, his expression thoughtful, considered the vastness of space before them. "It's a reminder of just how small we are in the grand scheme of things. But also how much potential there is for exploration and discovery."

"We should not forget our key purpose in coming to this place; we are here to meet our ancestors." Said Dr. Marcus.

As the spacecraft glided closer to the enigmatic planet H1009b, the tension onboard was palpable. Each member of the team felt a surge of anticipation mixed with a hint of trepidation. This was the moment they had been preparing for—the culmination of months of planning and anticipation.

Arius, her gaze fixed on the viewscreen, marveled at the sight before her. "It's incredible," she whispered, her voice barely above a murmur. "To think that we're finally here, on the brink of unraveling one of the greatest mysteries of our time."

Lyra, her fingers dancing across the control panel, nodded in agreement. "Indeed, Arius. But let's not forget that caution is our greatest ally here. We must proceed carefully, lest we disturb the delicate balance of this ancient world."

Dr. Sarah, her eyes scanning the data readouts, chimed in with a note of caution. "Agreed, Lyra. We must approach this with the utmost care. We don't yet know what awaits us on the surface of this planet."

Rian, his hands steady on the controls, nodded in agreement. "We'll proceed with caution but also with determination. We've come too far to turn back now."

Elena, with her focus on the navigational charts, spoke up with a sense of determination. "We'll need to find a suitable landing site, one that offers us the best chance of making contact with any inhabitants that may reside here."

Dr. Marcus, his eyes scanning the horizon, offered a word of reassurance. "We're ready for whatever challenges may come our way. Together, we'll navigate this unknown terrain and unlock the secrets that lie hidden beneath its surface."

After meticulous scans and analysis, the team identified a promising site for their descent—a vast expanse of flat terrain nestled between towering rock formations, bathed in the soft glow of the planet's twin moons. It seemed like an ideal location, offering both ample space for the spacecraft's landing and potential shelter from any unexpected hazards.

As the spacecraft descended towards the chosen landing site, the tension onboard reached its peak. Each member of the team held their breath, their eyes fixed on the viewscreen, as the landscape below grew steadily closer. The hum of the engines filled the air, a steady thrumming that echoed the rapid beating of their hearts.

With practiced precision, Rian guided the spacecraft towards the surface, his hands steady on the controls. Elena monitored their descent, *her expert calculations ensuring a smooth touchdown. Dr. Marcus and his team stood ready, prepared to spring into action at a moment's notice should anything go awry.*

As the spacecraft touched down on the surface of H1000b with a soft thud, a collective sigh of relief echoed through the cabin. They had made it safely to the planet's surface; their journey thus far is a testament to their skill and determination.

As the team stepped out onto the terrain, their spacesuits providing a barrier against the unfamiliar atmosphere, they were immediately struck by the awe-inspiring landscapes that stretched out before them. Towering rock formations carved by eons of wind and water, vast plains dotted with strange flora, and distant mountains shrouded in mist—all painted a picture of a world teeming with ancient mysteries waiting to be uncovered.

Their senses heightened by the novelty of their surroundings, the team moved cautiously, their eyes scanning the horizon for any signs of life or activity. It was then that they noticed a peculiar sight—a sleek, futuristic vehicle soaring through the sky towards them with effortless grace.

As the vehicle descended to the ground nearby, the team watched in astonishment as a figure emerged from within, clad in attire that seemed both familiar and yet distinctly alien. With a sense of curiosity and trepidation, they waited as the figure approached, unsure of what to expect from this unexpected encounter.

As the figure drew closer, it became apparent that their appearance was indeed reminiscent of the ancient human forms depicted in the historical records the team had studied. Clad in garments that bore markings and symbols reminiscent of a bygone era, the individual exuded an aura of wisdom and authority that commanded respect.

"Welcome, travelers," the figure greeted them, their voice echoing with a melodic resonance that seemed to transcend language barriers. "I am Kael, the Guardian of the Ancients. It is an honor to meet you."

Dr. Arius stepped forward, her demeanor poised yet curious. "We come in peace, Kael," she replied, her voice steady despite the underlying tension. "We seek to learn more about our ancestors and their connection to this world."

Kael regarded them with a knowing gaze, as if sensing the weight of their intentions. "You are not the first to come seeking answers," they remarked cryptically. "But perhaps you are the ones destined to uncover the truths that lie buried beneath the sands of time."

With that enigmatic pronouncement, Kael gestured towards the waiting vehicle, inviting the team to follow. "Come," they said, their tone imbued with a sense of urgency. "There is much to discuss and little time to waste."

The flying car soared gracefully through the skies, carrying the team and Kael towards the heart of the ancient city. As they traversed the landscape, Dr. Arius couldn't help but marvel at the blend of modern technology and ancient architecture that surrounded them, a testament to the resilience and ingenuity of the ancient humans.

Upon arriving at the main government office, the team was greeted by a delegation of officials adorned in ceremonial robes, their faces etched with a sense of reverence and respect. Kael led them through the grand entrance, where they were ushered into a spacious chamber filled with ornate furnishings and shimmering tapestries.

As the team settled into the grandeur of the government office, a figure emerged from the shadows, his presence commanding attention. Dr. Aviyaan Murphy, a renowned astrophysicist and biologist, stepped forward, his eyes alight with curiosity and intellect.

"Dr. Aviyaan Murphy," Kael announced, his voice reverent. "He is one of our most esteemed scientists, with expertise in astrophysics and biology, and a keeper of our ancient lore and wisdom."

Dr. Murphy nodded in greeting, his demeanor both welcoming and enigmatic. "Greetings, travelers," he said, his voice resonating with knowledge and experience. "I am the scientist who led this civilization to this planet, as the conditions on Earth at that time were not so habitable for us."

"That's impressive," remarked Dr. Arius Nova.

"We left a DNA-encrypted message on Earth," Dr. Aviyaan Murphy explained.

"Yes, we managed to decode it," Dr. Rian confirmed.

Dr. Marcus elaborated, "Our mission was to contact your civilization. We left Earth, reached near Neptune, encountered aliens, escaped from them, created a wormhole, and arrived here."

Dr. Murphy's eyes widened with intrigue as he listened to their journey. "Your endeavor is nothing short of remarkable. It seems fate has woven our paths together once more."

The team felt a sense of awe and accomplishment, realizing they had achieved their primary mission. Now, with Dr. Aviyaan

Murphy's guidance, they could delve deeper into the history and future of their civilizations, united by a common heritage and an enduring quest for knowledge.

Dr. Murphy led them into a grand hall adorned with intricate murals and advanced technology seamlessly integrated into the architecture. "This is our Hall of Knowledge," he explained. "Here, we preserve the history of our journey from Earth and the advancements we've made on this planet. It is also a place where we welcome visitors like yourselves who seek to bridge the gap between our worlds."

As they walked through the hall, Dr. Murphy pointed out various artifacts and displays that chronicled their civilization's development. The team marveled at the blend of human ingenuity and the alien world's resources, which had allowed their ancestors to thrive in this new environment.

Dr. Elena, her eyes wide with wonder, asked, "How did you manage to adapt so well to this planet?"

Dr. Murphy smiled. "It was not without its challenges. Our biologists and engineers, much *like yourselves, worked tirelessly to understand the planet's ecosystem and harness its resources. We developed technologies that allowed us to thrive, and we integrated our knowledge of Earth's biosphere with the new elements we discovered here."*

Dr. Lyra, fascinated by the technological advancements, inquired, "What about the integration of human biology with the alien environment? How did you manage that?"

"Our geneticists, including myself, focused on enhancing our resilience to the new environment," Dr. Murphy explained. "We made subtle modifications to our DNA to better suit the conditions here, ensuring that we could survive and flourish. It was a delicate balance, but one that we achieved with great care and precision."

As the conversation continued, the team felt a profound connection to their ancestors. They realized that, despite the vast distance and the many years that had separated them, the core essence of humanity's spirit of exploration and adaptation remained unchanged. They had come full circle, uniting two branches of humanity that had diverged but now stood together once more.

"We've made significant advancements," Dr. Murphy began, "but one of our most pressing challenges has always been establishing a stable and permanent connection with other worlds, especially Earth. Given your recent journey and your success with the wormhole, it seems we are closer than ever to achieving this goal."

Dr. Arius, her mind already buzzing with possibilities, leaned forward. "Our temporary wormhole was a success, but it was highly unstable. We need to find a way to make it a lasting and reliable pathway."

Dr. Murphy nodded. "Precisely. A permanent wormhole would not only facilitate travel but also ensure a continuous exchange of knowledge and resources. It would be a bridge between our civilizations, uniting us in ways previously unimaginable."

Dr. Rian, ever the strategist, added, "The key will be ensuring the stability of the wormhole. The fluctuations in space-time fabric are unpredictable, and we need a way to control and stabilize them."

Dr. Elena chimed in, "Our current understanding is limited, but with your advanced knowledge and our recent experiences, we might be able to devise a solution. What if we could create a dual-anchor system? One anchor here and one on Earth, both equipped with synchronized stabilization mechanisms."

Dr. Murphy's eyes sparkled with interest. "A dual-anchor system could work, but it would require immense energy and precise synchronization. We would need to harness both antimatter and dark matter to create a stable flow of energy between the two points."

Dr. Marcus suggested the installation of power stations at both entry points of the wormhole. This setup would ensure a consistent and reliable supply of power, thereby enhancing its operational security and stability.

SEVEN
ENCOUNTER

Meanwhile, as the scientists deliberated on the logistics of the wormhole project, the tranquility of H1009b was shattered by the sudden appearance of V'reth ships in the planet's orbit. The sleek, formidable vessels cast ominous shadows over the surface, their presence signaling imminent danger.

Dr. Arius Nova, alerted by the readings from the AWSRA spacecraft's sensors, immediately called for a security briefing. "We must prepare for potential conflict," she declared, her voice tinged with urgency. "The V'reth have followed us here, and their intentions are clear."

The team gathered in the command center, their faces set in grim determination. "What are our options?" Dr. Sarah Dax asked, her expression reflecting concern for the inhabitants of H1009b.

Dr. Rian, reviewing tactical data on the viewscreen, responded, "Our best chance is to defend ourselves and the inhabitants. We have the laser gun and our spacecraft's defenses, but we're outnumbered. We need a strategy."

"We could attempt to negotiate," suggested Dr. Lyra, her voice steady despite the tension in the room. "Maybe there's a way to communicate with them peacefully."

Before Dr. Arius could respond, the viewscreen flickered to life, displaying an incoming transmission from the lead V'reth ship. The alien commander's voice boomed through the speakers, filled with authority and threat.

"Humans of AWSRA," the V'reth commander began, "you have trespassed into our territory. Surrender immediately or face annihilation. We will not tolerate interference in our affairs."

Dr. Marcus clenched his fists, his resolve unwavering. "We can't surrender," he asserted. "Not after everything we've worked for."

A tense silence fell over the room as the gravity of their situation sank in. On one side, the AWSRA team stood united, determined to protect their mission and the inhabitants of H1009b. On the other hand, the V'reth, powerful and unyielding, posed a formidable threat.

"We need to buy time," Dr. Arius finally said.

As the situation grew dire, Marcus's voice broke through the tension. "I have an idea. What if we use the laser gun to create a temporary energy barrier?"

"A shield?" Elena inquired, intrigued by the possibility.

Marcus nodded. "Exactly. It won't hold forever, but it might buy us enough time to regroup and come up with a better strategy."

Arius considered the proposal for a moment before nodding in agreement. "Do it, Marcus.

Let's buy ourselves some breathing room."

With focused determination, Marcus recalibrated the laser gun, redirecting its output to create a protective energy shield around the AWSRA spacecraft. The shield shimmered into existence just in time to deflect a barrage of energy blasts from the V'reth ships.

In a few minutes, the V'reth's cracked the shield.

"We're under attack!" Dr. Arius exclaimed, her voice edged with urgency. "Prepare the defenses! Dr. Marcus, ready the laser gun on our spacecraft. Dr. Rian, coordinate with H1009b's defense forces."

Outside, the skies above H1009b swiftly filled with the graceful yet deadly warships of the planet's defense fleet. These ships, advanced and formidable, maneuvered into position to intercept the aggressive V'reth attackers. Dr. Aviyaan Murphy, known for his steady demeanor in times of crisis, stepped forward. "We have anticipated this scenario. Our defense fleet is equipped to handle such threats. Let's show them the strength of our alliance."

As the V'reth fleet recoiled from the devastating blow inflicted by H1009b's defense forces, the AWSRA team and their allies seized the opportunity to press their advantage. Dr. Arius Nova's voice cut through the chaos, her commands echoing with urgency amidst the din of battle.

"Continue the assault! Do not let them regroup!" she ordered, her eyes fixed on the dwindling enemy forces.

Dr. Marcus, his hands steady on the controls of the laser gun, unleashed a barrage of concentrated energy towards the retreating V'reth ships. Each shot was meticulously aimed, targeting critical systems and forcing the alien vessels into evasive maneuvers.

Dr. Aviyaan Murphy, observing the battle unfold with a blend of caution and resolve, monitored the fleet's movements. "They're scattering," he noted, his voice echoing through the control room. "Their formation is breaking. We have them on the run."

The warships of H1009b, guided by skilled pilots and armed with cutting-edge weaponry, maintained relentless pressure on the V'reth.

Plasma bursts and energy beams filled the void of space as the battle reached its climax. Despite the V'reth's technological prowess, they found themselves overwhelmed by the unified defense efforts of H1009b and the Earth team.

"We can't let them escape!" Dr. Rian urged his strategic mind to focus on exploiting every advantage. "Coordinate with the fleet. Pursue and eliminate their stragglers."

Elena, navigating the AWSRA spacecraft amidst the chaos, adjusted their position to support the allied fleet's movements. "Track remaining hostiles. They're attempting to retreat towards their own territory," she reported, her voice steady despite the intensity of the situation.

With coordinated precision, the combined forces of H1009b and the AWSRA team harried the remaining V'reth ships, preventing any chance of a counterattack. Soon, the enemy vessels, battered and reeling from the fierce engagement, vanished into the darkness of space, their retreat an acknowledgment of defeat.

As the battle subsided, a palpable sense of relief swept through the control room. The team exchanged glances, their expressions a mix of exhaustion and triumph. Dr. Arius Nova's voice rang out, cutting through the tension that lingered.

As the echoes of battle subsided in the vast expanse of space, Dr. Arius Nova turned to her team, a mixture of relief and determination on her face. "We've held them off for now, but we can't afford to let our guard down. Dr. Rian, get in touch with Earth. We need to confirm that our mission here on H1009b, codenamed 'Origins', has been a success."

Dr. Rian nodded, his fingers swiftly dancing across the communication console. After a tense moment, a connection was established with Earth Command.

"This is Dr. Rian of the AWSRA mission," he began, his voice steady despite the weariness that crept in after the intense battle. "We have successfully reached H1009b and made contact with its inhabitants. The mission to establish a connection with our ancient ancestors has begun."

The response from Earth was swift and relieved. "Acknowledged, Dr. Rian. We've been monitoring the situation. Your success is crucial to our understanding of our origins and the future of interstellar cooperation."

Dr. Arius glanced around the control room, a sense of pride swelling within her. "Our work here is far from over," she announced to her team. "But today, we've made history. Let's ensure that our alliance with H1009b grows stronger and that the dual-anchor system for the wormhole becomes a reality."

Dr. Aviyaan Murphy, ever the cautious optimist, added, "Indeed, this is just the beginning. The V'reth will not be the last challenge we face, but together, we have proven that unity and determination can overcome even the most formidable obstacles."

As the team on H1009b prepared for the next phase of their mission, the distant stars shimmered with promise and possibility. The journey to uncover the mysteries of their shared origins had only just begun.

FIVE YEARS LATER:

Five years had passed since the AWSRA team successfully stabilized the wormhole between Earth and H1009b, ushering in a new era of interstellar cooperation. The team, hailed as heroes, returned to Earth amidst fanfare and celebration. Media outlets broadcasted their achievements, and public curiosity surged about the newfound civilization beyond the wormhole.

Dr. Arius Nova stood on the balcony of the AWSRA headquarters, overlooking the bustling cityscape below. The skyline shimmered with a blend of futuristic architecture and traditional landmarks, a testament to humanity's resilience and innovation. She took a deep breath, reflecting on the journey that had brought them here—the challenges, the victories, and the profound discoveries.

Inside the headquarters, Dr. Marcus and Dr. Elena worked tirelessly in the newly established command center. The dual-anchor system they had devised proved robust, ensuring a stable flow of energy through the wormhole. Regular exchanges of knowledge, culture, and technology flourished between Earth and

H1009b, enriching both civilizations.

In a grand diplomatic gesture, governments on both sides of the wormhole scheduled a historic meeting. Diplomatic envoys and scientists prepared meticulously for the event, eager to forge formal ties and outline mutual cooperation agreements. The meeting represented a pivotal moment in human history, bridging worlds separated by vast distances and time.

Dr. Aviyaan Murphy, now a revered figure on both Earth and H1009b, addressed a gathering of scientists and diplomats. His words resonated with optimism and hope for the future. "We stand on the threshold of a new age," he declared, his voice carrying across the assembly. "Together, we have shown that curiosity and collaboration can transcend even the most daunting challenges."

As the meeting concluded, members of the AWSRA team gathered for a quiet moment of reflection. Dr. Rian, always the strategist, contemplated the implications of their discoveries for interstellar diplomacy. "This is just the beginning," he mused, his gaze fixed on the distant stars visible through the window. "There's so much more to explore, so much more to learn."

Dr. Marcus looked at his colleagues and the vast universe beyond, his voice filled with hope. "In the meeting of minds, we find the bridge to a shared future."

With these words echoing in their hearts, the team knew that their journey was far from over. The exploration, the learning, and the building of bridges between worlds would continue, fueled by the unwavering spirit of humanity and the bonds they had forged.

In the vast expanse of space, amidst the infinite possibilities of the cosmos, humanity had found a new beginning. The stars beckoned, and united by their shared dreams and discoveries, they stepped boldly into the future.

Charecter Biographies

Dr. Arius Nova:

Name: *Dr. Arius Nova*

Occupation: *Lead Scientist at the Advanced Wormhole Stabilization and Research Agency (AWSRA)*

Age: *45*

Nationality: *Earth-born, Global Citizen*

Physical Description: *Dr. Arius Nova stands at 5'9" with a lean, athletic build, indicative of her active lifestyle. She has piercing green eyes that convey her intense focus and determination. Her shoulder-length auburn hair is often tied back in a practical style that suits her hands-on approach to her work. Her high cheekbones, sharp jawline, and determined expression contribute to her authoritative presence.*

Personality Traits:

Intelligent: *Dr. Nova's intellectual capabilities are extraordinary. Her ability to think several steps ahead allows her to solve complex problems and anticipate future challenges. Her strategic mind has been crucial to the successful stabilization of the wormhole.*

Determined: *Once Dr. Nova sets her mind on a goal, she is relentless in her pursuit. This tenacity has driven her to overcome numerous scientific and bureaucratic obstacles throughout her career.*

Empathetic: *Despite her intense focus on her work, Dr. Nova is deeply empathetic, caring about her team and the well-being of humanity. Her empathy makes her a beloved leader and an effective collaborator.*

Resilient: *Dr. Nova has faced and overcome significant personal and professional hardships, emerging stronger each time. Her resilience inspires those around her to persevere, no matter the odds.*

Education: *Dr. Nova holds multiple advanced*

degrees in physics, astrophysics, and engineering from prestigious institutions. She completed her Ph.D. in quantum mechanics with a focus on wormhole theory at the age of 28, impressing her mentors and peers with her groundbreaking dissertation.

Background: *Born into a family of scientists, Arius Nova was exposed to the wonders of the cosmos from a young age. Her parents, both renowned researchers, nurtured her curiosity and provided her with the resources to explore her passions. She excelled academically, showing a particular aptitude for physics and mathematics.*

Her early career was marked by groundbreaking research in quantum mechanics, which earned her several awards and recognitions. However, it was her work on wormhole theory that truly set her apart. Her innovative ideas caught the attention of the AWSRA, and she was soon recruited to lead their most ambitious project yet: stabilizing a wormhole between Earth and the distant planet H1009b.

Career Highlights:

Quantum Mechanics Research: Dr. Nova's early work in quantum mechanics laid the foundation for her later achievements. Her research provided new insights into the behavior of particles at the quantum level and challenged existing paradigms in the field.

Wormhole Stabilization: As the lead scientist at AWSRA, Dr. Nova was instrumental in the successful stabilization of the wormhole. Her expertise in quantum mechanics and engineering enabled her team to devise the dual-anchor system that ensured the wormhole's stability.

Interstellar Diplomat: In addition to her scientific achievements, Dr. Nova played a key role in fostering cooperation between Earth and H1009b. Her diplomatic skills and empathetic nature helped bridge the gap between the two civilizations, paving the way for future collaboration.

Significant Projects and Contributions:

The Quantum Anchor Project: Dr. Nova led the development of the quantum anchor, a revolutionary technology that stabilizes the wormhole by anchoring it to specific quantum coordinates on both Earth and H1009b. This project was a pivotal moment in interstellar travel, making consistent and safe passage possible.

Interstellar Communication Network: *Understanding the need for constant and reliable communication, Dr. Nova spearheaded the creation of an advanced interstellar communication network. This system allowed real-time data exchange and video communication between Earth and H1009b, significantly enhancing cooperation and cultural exchange.*

Cultural Exchange Programs: *Recognizing the importance of understanding and integrating the cultures of H1009b, Dr. Nova initiated various cultural exchange programs. These programs facilitated the sharing of knowledge, traditions, and innovations, fostering mutual respect and understanding between the two worlds.*

Personal Life: *Despite her demanding career, Dr. Nova makes time for her personal interests. She is an avid reader, particularly of science fiction, which she credits with inspiring many of her early ideas. She enjoys hiking and stargazing, activities that allow her to connect* *with the natural world and the universe she studies so passionately. Dr. Nova is also known for her love of music, often playing the piano to unwind after a long day.*

Family and Relationships: *Dr. Nova's family has always been a source of support and inspiration. Her parents, both retired scientists, remain her biggest supporters. She shares a close bond with her younger brother, an environmental scientist working on climate change solutions. Dr. Nova's personal relationships, while fewer due to her career commitments, are deep and meaningful. She maintains close friendships with her colleagues and former students, often mentoring them in their own scientific pursuits.*

Legacy: *Dr. Arius Nova's contributions to science and humanity are immeasurable. She not only advanced our understanding of the universe but also helped secure a future where Earth and H1009b can coexist and thrive. Her work continues to inspire future generations of scientists, explorers, and dreamers. Her legacy is not just in her scientific achievements but also in her ability to bring people together, fostering collaboration and unity in the face of daunting challenges.*

Dr. Rian Dax:

Name: Dr. Rian Dax

Occupation: Strategic Analyst and Diplomat at the Advanced Wormhole Stabilization and Research Agency (AWSRA)

Age: 42

Nationality: Earth-born, Global Citizen

Physical Description: Dr. Rian Dax stands at 6'1" with a lean but muscular build, a result of his disciplined approach to fitness. He has deep blue eyes that are often alight with curiosity and intelligence. His short-cropped black hair and a neatly trimmed beard give him a distinguished, authoritative appearance. His composed demeanor and sharp features make him a compelling presence in any room.

Personality Traits:

Analytical: Dr. Dax is known for his exceptional analytical abilities. He excels at dissecting *complex problems and devising strategic solutions, making him invaluable in both scientific and diplomatic endeavors.*

Calm Under Pressure: *Even in the most stressful situations, Dr. Dax remains unflappable. His calm demeanor and ability to think clearly under pressure have earned him the respect of his colleagues and the trust of those he negotiates with.*

Diplomatic: *With a natural talent for diplomacy, Dr. Dax is skilled at navigating political landscapes and fostering cooperation between diverse groups. His diplomatic efforts have been crucial in establishing and maintaining interstellar relations.*

Innovative: *Dr. Dax constantly seeks new and creative solutions to challenges. His innovative thinking has led to significant advancements in strategic planning and interstellar diplomacy.*

Education: *Dr. Dax holds advanced degrees in political science, strategic studies, and astrophysics from leading universities around the world. He completed his Ph.D. in interstellar diplomacy, focusing on the theoretical frameworks necessary for peaceful and* *productive interstellar relations.*

Background: *Born into a family with a strong military and academic tradition, Rian Dax was groomed for greatness from an early age. His father, a decorated military strategist, and his mother, a renowned astrophysicist, instilled in him a deep sense of duty and a love for learning. Excelling in both academics and athletics, he developed a keen interest in the intersection of science and strategy.*

His early career saw him working in various capacities within international organizations, where he honed his skills in negotiation and strategic analysis. His unique combination of scientific knowledge and strategic acumen quickly set him apart, leading to his recruitment by the AWSRA.

Career Highlights:

Strategic Planning: *Dr. Dax played a pivotal role in the strategic planning of the AWSRA's mission to stabilize the wormhole. His foresight and detailed contingency plans were instrumental in the mission's success.*

Diplomatic Negotiations: *His diplomatic skills were crucial in the negotiations with the inhabitants of H1009b. Dr. Dax's ability to build trust and foster cooperation ensured a smooth integration of interstellar relations.*

Conflict Resolution: *Dr. Dax's expertise in conflict resolution was tested during the V'reth attack on H1009b. His strategic decisions and calm leadership helped turn the tide of the battle and secure a victory for the allied forces.*

Significant Projects and Contributions:

Wormhole Security Protocols: *Dr. Dax developed comprehensive security protocols for the wormhole, ensuring safe and controlled passage between Earth and H1009b. His protocols have become the gold standard for interstellar travel.*

Cultural Integration Programs: *Understanding the importance of cultural exchange, Dr. Dax initiated programs that facilitated the sharing of knowledge, traditions, and customs between Earth and H1009b. These programs have been essential in building mutual respect and understanding.*

Interstellar Conflict Mediation: *Dr. Dax has been instrumental in mediating conflicts not only between Earth and H1009b but also within their respective societies. His ability to find common ground and propose equitable solutions has prevented numerous potential conflicts.*

Personal Life: *Dr. Dax is a man of varied interests. Outside of his professional responsibilities, he enjoys reading extensively on philosophy, history, and science fiction. An avid chess player, he appreciates the strategic depth of the game, often engaging in matches with colleagues and friends. He also practices martial arts, valuing the discipline and physical fitness it provides.*

Family and Relationships: *Dr. Dax maintains close ties with his family, particularly his parents, who continue to inspire him with their achievements. He is also very close to his sister, an environmental lawyer working on sustainability issues. Though his demanding career leaves little time for personal relationships, Dr. Dax values the deep connections he has with his colleagues, whom he considers extended family. His mentorship of younger scientists and diplomats is particularly notable, as he takes great pride in nurturing the* *next generation of leaders.*

Legacy: Dr. Rian Dax's legacy is one of strategic brilliance and diplomatic finesse. His contributions have not only advanced humanity's understanding of interstellar relations but also ensured a peaceful and prosperous future for Earth and H1009b. His work continues to inspire those who strive to bridge the gap between science and diplomacy, proving that with intelligence, calmness, and cooperation, even the most complex challenges can be overcome.

DR. AVIYAAN MURPHY:

Name: *Dr. Aviyaan Murphy*

Occupation: *Lead Scientist and Diplomat at the Earth Welfare Society (EWS)*

Age: *45*

Nationality: *Earth-born, Global Citizen*

Physical Description: *Dr. Aviyaan Murphy is*

a tall, imposing figure at 6'3", with a robust build that speaks of years of rigorous fieldwork and dedication to his profession. His piercing green eyes, often alight with curiosity and determination, contrast with his short, silver-streaked hair. A neatly trimmed beard adds to his distinguished and authoritative appearance. His presence exudes confidence and command, making him a natural leader.

Personality Traits:

Visionary: Dr. Murphy is known for his forward-thinking approach and ability to envision innovative solutions to complex problems. His visionary mindset has driven many of the EWS's groundbreaking initiatives.

Resilient: Having faced numerous challenges in his career, Dr. Murphy possesses unyielding resilience. He remains steadfast in his goals, inspiring his team to persevere through adversity.

Empathetic: *Despite his commanding presence, Dr. Murphy is deeply empathetic. He values the well-being of his team and the communities he serves, often going to great lengths to ensure their needs are met.*

Charismatic: *His natural charisma and eloquence make him an effective communicator and diplomat. He easily gains the trust and respect of those around him, whether in scientific circles or diplomatic meetings.*

Education: *Dr. Murphy holds a doctorate in astrobiology and interstellar diplomacy from a prestigious global university. His multidisciplinary education combines advanced scientific knowledge with expertise in diplomatic relations, uniquely positioning him to lead interstellar initiatives.*

Background: *Aviyaan Murphy was born into a family of scholars and explorers. His parents, both renowned scientists, instilled in him a love for discovery and a deep sense of responsibility towards humanity's future. From an early age, Aviyaan showed an exceptional aptitude for science and diplomacy, often mediating conflicts among peers and devising innovative solutions to scientific problems.*

His early career saw him working with various international research organizations, where he quickly rose through the ranks due to his exceptional skills and dedication. His work on sustainable technologies and interstellar communication garnered global recognition, leading to his pivotal role in the Earth Welfare Society.

Career Highlights:

Wormhole Stabilization: *Dr. Murphy led the AWSRA team in successfully stabilizing the wormhole between Earth and H1009b. This achievement not only prevented ecological collapse on Earth but also opened new frontiers for interstellar cooperation.*

Interstellar Diplomacy: *As a diplomat, Dr. Murphy played a crucial role in establishing and maintaining peaceful relations with the inhabitants of H1009b. His efforts laid the foundation for a historic alliance that benefits both civilizations.*

Crisis Management: *During the V'reth attack on H1009b, Dr. Murphy's leadership and strategic acumen were instrumental in* *coordinating the defense efforts, ultimately securing a victory for the allied forces.*

Significant Projects and Contributions:

Environmental Restoration: *Dr. Murphy spearheaded numerous projects aimed at restoring Earth's ecosystems, using advanced technologies and knowledge gained from interstellar exchanges.*

Cultural Exchange Programs: *He initiated and oversaw cultural exchange programs that facilitated the sharing of knowledge, traditions, and innovations between Earth and H1009b. These programs have significantly enriched both societies.*

Advanced Research Facilities: *Under his leadership, the EWS established cutting-edge research facilities dedicated to exploring new scientific frontiers and developing sustainable technologies.*

Personal Life: *Outside of his professional commitments, Dr. Murphy is an avid nature enthusiast. He enjoys spending time in natural reserves, often engaging in activities like hiking* and bird-watching. He also has a passion for classical music and can often be found playing the piano during his leisure time.

Family and Relationships: Dr. Murphy maintains a close relationship with his family, who continue to be his source of inspiration. He is particularly close to his younger brother, who is a pioneering environmental scientist. Despite his demanding career, he values quality time with his loved ones and ensures he remains an active part of their lives.

Legacy: Dr. Aviyaan Murphy's legacy is defined by his remarkable contributions to science and diplomacy. His visionary leadership and unwavering commitment to humanity's future have set a precedent for future generations. Through his work, he has not only safeguarded Earth's ecological stability but also forged a path for interstellar collaboration, proving that unity and innovation are the keys to overcoming even the greatest challenges.

Dr. Lyra Nova:

Name: Dr. Lyra Nova

Occupation: *Chief Scientist and Astrophysicist at the Earth Welfare Society (EWS)*

Age: *38*

Nationality: *Earth-born, International Citizen*

Physical Description: *Dr. Lyra Nova is a striking figure with a height of 5'9". She has a light and agile build, honed by years of field research and exploration. Her piercing blue eyes, always brimming with curiosity and intelligence, are her most notable feature. Lyra's long, chestnut-brown hair is usually tied back in a practical ponytail, and her attire is a blend of functional and professional, reflecting her readiness for both lab work and diplomatic engagements.*

Personality Traits:

Brilliant: *Dr. Nova is known for her exceptional intellect and problem-solving skills. Her innovative thinking has led to numerous breakthroughs in astrophysics and interstellar technology.*

Meticulous: *Her attention to detail is unparalleled, making her a meticulous scientist who leaves no stone unturned in her research and analysis.*

Compassionate: *Lyra is deeply compassionate, often putting the needs of her team and the greater good above her own. Her empathy extends to all living beings, driving her commitment to environmental and humanitarian causes.*

Determined: *Once she sets her mind on a goal, she is relentless in her pursuit. Her determination has helped her overcome numerous professional and personal challenges.*

Education: *Dr. Nova holds a Ph.D. in astronomy from one of the world's leading universities. She also has advanced degrees in environmental science and interstellar communication, equipping her with a broad and versatile skill set.*

Background: *Born into a family of scientists and explorers, Lyra's childhood was filled with stories of space and discovery. Her parents, both renowned astronomers, nurtured her innate curiosity and encouraged her to pursue her* *passions. As a young prodigy, Lyra excelled in her studies and was frequently involved in advanced scientific projects.*

Her early career involved extensive research on celestial phenomena and environmental sustainability. Her work attracted the attention of the Earth Welfare Society, where she quickly became an integral part of their scientific community.

Career Highlights:

Wormhole Exploration: *Dr. Nova played a pivotal role in exploring and stabilizing the wormhole between Earth and H1009b. Her expertise in astrophysics was crucial to understanding the complexities of the wormhole and ensuring safe passage.*

Planetary Defense: *During the V'reth attack on H1009b, her quick thinking and analytical skills were instrumental in coordinating defense strategies and mitigating damage.*

Scientific Collaboration: *She has been a key figure in fostering scientific collaboration between Earth and H1009b, facilitating the* exchange of knowledge and technological advancements.

Significant Projects and Contributions:

Sustainable Technologies: Lyra has led several projects focused on developing sustainable technologies to address Earth's ecological crisis. Her innovations have significantly contributed to environmental restoration efforts.

Interstellar Research Initiatives: She has initiated and overseen numerous interstellar research initiatives, expanding humanity's understanding of the universe and our place within it.

Educational Outreach: Dr. Nova is passionate about education and frequently engages in outreach programs to inspire the next generation of scientists and explorers.

Personal Life: Dr. Nova is an avid reader and enjoys immersing herself in both scientific literature and classic novels. She has a love for music, often playing the violin in her free time. Lyra also enjoys hiking and stargazing, activities that allow her to connect with nature *and the cosmos.*

Family and Relationships: *Despite her demanding career, Lyra maintains strong connections with her family and friends. She often credits her parents for her scientific curiosity and moral compass. Lyra values deep, meaningful relationships and is known for being a supportive and loyal friend.*

Legacy: *Dr. Lyra Voss's legacy is one of brilliance, compassion, and unwavering dedication to the betterment of humanity and the universe. Her groundbreaking work in astrophysics and sustainability has left an indelible mark on the scientific community. Through her efforts, she has helped bridge the gap between Earth and H1009b, fostering a future of shared knowledge and cooperation. Lyra's life and career continue to inspire countless individuals to pursue their passions and make a positive impact on the world.*

DR. SARAH DAX:

Name: *Dr. Sarah Dax*

Occupation: *Chief Medical Officer and*

Biotechnologist at the Earth Welfare Society (EWS)

Age: 41

Nationality: Earth-born, International Citizen

Physical Description: Dr. Sarah Dax is a commanding presence, standing at 5'10" with an athletic build that speaks to his active lifestyle. His green eyes are sharp and perceptive, often reflecting her analytical mind. He has short, auburn hair that is usually kept in a practical style. His professional attire is always immaculate, blending functionality with a touch of elegance.

Personality Traits:

Compassionate: Sarah's primary motivation is the well-being of others. His empathy drives her work in medicine and biotechnology, where she is constantly striving to improve and save lives.

Resilient: He has faced numerous personal and professional challenges with grace and fortitude, never allowing setbacks to deter him *from his goals.*

Innovative: *Dr. Dax is known for his ability to think outside the box, developing novel solutions to complex medical and biological problem***Leadership:** *A natural leader, Sarah is both authoritative and approachable. He inspires confidence and trust in her team, fostering a collaborative and supportive environment.*

Education: *Sarah holds an M.D. with a specialization in internal medicine from a prestigious medical school. He also has a Ph.D. in biotechnology, focusing on genetic engineering and regenerative medicine.*

Background: *Sarah grew up in a family deeply rooted in the medical field. His parents were both doctors, and their commitment to patient care and medical ethics profoundly influenced him. From a young age, he was fascinated by the complexities of the human body and the potential of medical science to transform lives.*

Her early career involved working in high-pressure environments such as emergency rooms and intensive care units, where she honed her skills and developed a deep sense of empathy.

Later, her interest in biotechnology led her to groundbreaking research in genetic therapies and regenerative medicine.

Career Highlights:

Medical Innovations: *Dr. Dax has developed several pioneering treatments that have revolutionized patient care. His work in genetic therapy has provided cures for previously incurable diseases.*

Interstellar Medicine: *His expertise was crucial during the mission to H1009b, where she adapted Earth-based medical practices to the alien environment and developed new treatments for previously unknown conditions.*

Crisis Management: *Sarah's leadership and medical expertise were vital during the V'reth attack on H1009b, where she coordinated medical response efforts, saving countless lives.*

Significant Projects and Contributions:

Genetic Engineering: *He has led research projects that advanced the field of genetic* *engineering, creating therapies that have saved millions of lives and improved the quality of life for countless others.*

Regenerative Medicine: *His work in stem cell research and tissue regeneration has opened new frontiers in medicine, allowing for the repair and replacement of damaged tissues and organs.*

Interdisciplinary Collaboration: *Sarah has worked closely with scientists from various fields to integrate medical science with technology and environmental studies, fostering holistic approaches to health and wellness.*

Personal Life: *Sarah enjoys a variety of hobbies that help him maintain a balanced life. He is an avid runner, often participating in marathons. He also has a passion for painting, finding solace and expression through it. Despite her busy schedule, she makes time for her family and friends, valuing the deep connections she has built over the years.*

Legacy: *Dr. Sarah Dax's legacy is characterized by his relentless pursuit of medical excellence and his profound compassion for humanity. His* *groundbreaking work in biotechnology and medicine has left an indelible mark on the field, saving lives and offering hope where there was none. Through his leadership and innovative spirit, he has inspired a new generation of medical professionals to push the boundaries of what is possible, ensuring that her contributions will benefit humanity for generations to come.*

Dr. Marcus Dax:

Name: *Dr. Marcus Dax*

Occupation: *Chief Engineer and Astrophysicist at the Earth Welfare Society (EWS).*

Age: *45*

Nationality: *Earth-born, Global Citizen*

Physical Description: *Dr. Marcus Dax stands at 6'1" with a lean and athletic build. His dark brown hair is often tousled, a testament to the long hours spent in the lab and field. His piercing blue eyes are always observant, reflecting his analytical nature. Marcus often dresses in practical, comfortable attire suitable* *for both laboratory work and field expeditions.*

Personality Traits:

Analytical: *Marcus possesses a sharp intellect and excels in problem-solving, often tackling complex engineering and astrophysical challenges with ease.*

Innovative: *Known for his ability to think creatively, he is constantly devising new technologies and methods to advance space exploration and engineering.*

Determined: *His persistence and dedication to his work are unwavering, often pushing through obstacles and setbacks with a relentless drive.*

Collaborative: *Marcus values teamwork and is known for his ability to bring out the best in his colleagues, fostering an environment of cooperation and mutual respect.*

Education: *Marcus holds a Ph.D. in astronomy from a leading university, as well as a Master's degree in aerospace engineering. His* *educational background provides a strong foundation for his work in both theoretical and applied sciences.*

Background: *Growing up, Marcus was fascinated by the stars and the mechanics of how things worked. His parents, both engineers, nurtured his curiosity and provided him with the tools and knowledge to explore his interests. As a child, he built complex models and conducted experiments, laying the groundwork for his future career.*

His early professional years were spent working on space missions and developing advanced propulsion systems. His expertise in astrophysics and engineering quickly made him a valuable asset in the scientific community.

Career Highlights:

Space Exploration: *Dr. Dax has contributed to numerous space missions, developing innovative technologies that have enhanced humanity's ability to explore the cosmos.*

Wormhole Stabilization: *His work on stabilizing the wormhole between Earth and*

H1009b was crucial, ensuring safe and reliable travel between the two worlds.

Energy Systems: Marcus designed the dual-anchor system that maintains the stability of the wormhole, a feat of engineering that has revolutionized interstellar travel.

Significant Projects and Contributions:

Propulsion Systems: Marcus has developed advanced propulsion technologies that have increased the efficiency and range of space travel, enabling deeper exploration of the universe.

Wormhole Research: His pioneering research on wormhole physics and stabilization mechanisms has paved the way for safe interstellar travel, bridging vast distances between worlds.

Interdisciplinary Innovations: Marcus has collaborated with experts in various fields to integrate engineering, physics, and biology, resulting in groundbreaking advancements in space exploration and technology.

Personal Life: In his free time, Marcus enjoys stargazing, often spending nights under the open sky with his telescope. He is also an avid rock climber, finding both physical challenge and mental clarity in the activity. Despite his demanding career, he values spending time with his family and friends, often organizing gatherings that blend scientific curiosity with personal connections.

Family and Relationships: Dr. Marcus Dax is married to Dr. Sarah Dax, a distinguished medical officer and biotechnologist. Their partnership is built on mutual respect and a shared passion for science and discovery. They have two children, who are the center of their lives and a source of constant inspiration.

Legacy: Dr. Marcus Dax's legacy is one of innovation and exploration. His contributions to astrophysics and engineering have significantly advanced humanity's understanding and capabilities in space travel. Through his work on the wormhole stabilization project and other groundbreaking technologies, Marcus has left an indelible mark on the scientific community. His dedication to pushing the boundaries of what is possible continues to inspire future generations of engineers and scientists, ensuring that his influence will be felt *for many years to come.*

www.ingramcontent.com/pod-product-compliance
Lightning Source LLC
Chambersburg PA
CBHW021400150726
47989CB00005B/2332